Selected Stories by
W.W. JACOBS

Books in this Series:

Selected Stories by O. Henry
Selected Stories by Anton Chekhov
Selected Stories by Guy de Maupassant
Selected Stories by Mark Twain
Selected Stories by Edgar Allan Poe
Selected Stories by Rudyard Kipling
Selected Stories by Saki
Selected Stories by Oscar Wilde
Selected Stories by Honoré de Balzac
Selected Stories by Charles Dickens
Selected Stories by D.H. Lawrence
Selected Stories by H.G. Wells
Selected Stories by Jack London
Selected Stories by Joseph Conrad
Selected Stories by Leo Tolstoy
Selected Stories by Sir Arthur Conan Doyle
Selected Stories by James Joyce
Selected Stories by Virginia Woolf
Selected Stories by Thomas Hardy
Selected Stories by Fyodor Dostoyevsky
Selected Stories by Katherine Mansfield
Selected Stories by Wilkie Collins
Selected Stories by Robert Louis Stevenson
Selected Stories by Howard Pyle
Selected Stories by Jerome K. Jerome
Selected Stories by Sir Walter Scott
Selected Stories by H. Rider Haggard
Selected Stories by G.K. Chesterton
Selected Stories by Bram Stoker
Selected Stories by Henry James
Selected Stories by F. Scott Fitzgerald

Selected Stories by
W.W. JACOBS

Published by
Rupa Publications India Pvt. Ltd 2015
7/16, Ansari Road, Daryaganj
New Delhi 110002

Sales Centres:
Allahabad Bengaluru Chennai
Hyderabad Jaipur Kathmandu
Kolkata Mumbai

Selection and Introduction copyright © Terry O'Brien 2015

All rights reserved.
No part of this publication may be reproduced, transmitted,
or stored in a retrieval system, in any form or by any means,
electronic, mechanical, photocopying, recording or otherwise,
without the prior permission of the publisher.

ISBN: 978-81-291-3705-0

First impression 2015

10 9 8 7 6 5 4 3 2 1

Printed at Shree Maitrey Printech Pvt. Ltd., Noida

This book is sold subject to the condition that it shall not,
by way of trade or otherwise, be lent, resold, hired out, or otherwise
circulated, without the publisher's prior consent, in any form of binding or
cover other than that in which it is published.

CONTENTS

Introduction		*vii*
1	The Monkey's Paw	1
2	The Lady of the Barge	14
3	The Well	28
4	The Toll-House	42
5	A Change of Treatment	54
6	The Captain's Exploit	63
7	Contraband of War	72
8	A Black Affair	86
9	The Skipper of the 'Osprey'	101
10	A Golden Venture	113
11.	Bill's Paper Chase	126

INTRODUCTION

William Wymark Jacobs (8 September 1863–1 September 1943), better known as W.W. Jacobs, was a British author born in Wapping, London. He is most famous for his horror story, 'The Monkey's Paw'. However, he more often uses a humorous tone in his stories illustrating the lives of the working-class people he grew up around.

Jacobs's father worked as a dockhand and wharf manager on the South Devon wharf and Jacobs drew heavily on his father's experiences for many of his short stories about life at sea and on the docks of England.

While he might not have enjoyed the fame of more well-known contemporaries, Jacobs was equally a master of the macabre and the witty, often brilliantly employing the vernacular of the East End of London in his stories.

- Jacobs's most famous story, 'The Monkey's Paw' has been filmed and adapted for the stage numerous times. The story is about the danger of wishing. Even though Mr White feels content with his life, he nevertheless uses the monkey's paw to wish for money that he doesn't really need.
- 'The Lady of the Barge' is part of a collection of the same name published in 1902. This is one of Jacobs's humorous tales about the skipper of a ship and a lady passenger.
- A suspense mystery, 'The Well' slowly builds up to a most unexpected ending.

- Another of Jacobs's macabre tales, 'The Toll-House' is set in a house known to be haunted. Jacobs plays off four characters against one another to create the suspense and mystery that drive the story to its inevitable conclusion.
- 'A Change of Treatment' is one of Jacobs's early stories published in the collection *Many Cargoes* in 1896. A humorous story, it is an example of how Jacobs used a third person as narrator in many of his stories.
- 'The Captain's Exploit' is an amusing tale of a misadventure at sea, with one shipping vessel being mistaken for another.
- 'Contraband of War' is a humorous story about life at sea and how the crew of a ship fools its captain.
- 'A Black Affair' is one of the many stories where Jacobs skilfully uses his childhood experiences of the docks to bring out the accents and mannerisms of the sailors.
- 'The Skipper of the "Osprey"' is an entertaining story with a female lead. This is another one of Jacobs's stories set aboard a small ship.
- 'A Golden Venture' plays on one of Jacobs's favourite themes of human nature and greed.
- Once again set aboard a ship, 'Bill's Paper Chase' is a story about two clever old hands being outwitted by a greenhorn.

1

THE MONKEY'S PAW

Without, the night was cold and wet, but in the small parlor of Lakesnam Villa the blinds were drawn and the fire burned brightly. Father and son were at chess, the former, who possessed ideas about the game involving radical changes, putting his king into such sharp and unnecessary perils that it even provoked comment from the whitehaired old lady knitting placidly by the fire. 'Hark at the wind,' said Mr White, who, having seen a fatal mistake after it was too late, was amiably desirous of preventing his son from seeing it. 'I'm listening,' said the latter, grimly surveying the board as he stretched out his hand. 'Check.' 'I should hardly think that he'd come tonight,' said his father, with his hand poised over the board. 'Mate,' replied the son. 'That's the worst of living so far out,' bawled Mr White, with sudden and unlooked-for violence; 'of all the beastly, slushy, out-of-the-way places to live in, this is the worst. Pathway's a bog, and the road's a torrent. I don't know what people are thinking about. I suppose because only two houses on the road are let, they think it doesn't matter.'

'Never mind, dear,' said his wife soothingly; 'perhaps you'll win the next one.'

Mr White looked up sharply, just in time to intercept a knowing glance between mother and son. The words died away on his lips, and he hid a guilty grin in his thin grey beard.

'There he is,' said Herbert White, as the gate banged to loudly and heavy footsteps came toward the door.

The old man rose with hospitable haste, and opening the door, was heard condoling with the new arrival. The new arrival also condoled with himself, so that Mrs White said, 'Tut, tut!' and coughed gently as her husband entered the room, followed by a tall, burly man, beady of eye and rubicund of visage.

'Sergeant Major Morris,' he said, introducing him.

The sergeant major shook hands, and taking the proffered seat by the fire, watched contentedly while his host got out whisky and tumblers and stood a small copper kettle on the fire.

At the third glass his eyes got brighter, and he began to talk, the little family circle regarding with eager interest this visitor from distant parts, as he squared his broad shoulders in the chair and spoke of strange scenes and doughty deeds, of wars and plagues and strange peoples.

'Twenty-one years of it,' said Mr White, nodding at his wife and son. 'When he went away he was a slip of a youth in the warehouse. Now look at him.'

'He don't look to have taken much harm,' said Mrs White politely. 'I'd like to go to India myself,' said the old man, 'just to look round a bit, you know.'

'Better where you are,' said the sergeant major, shaking his head. He put down the empty glass, and sighing softly, shook it again.

'I should like to see those old temples and fakirs and jugglers,' said the old man. 'What was that you started telling me the other day about a monkey's paw or something, Morris?'

'Nothing,' said the soldier hastily. 'Leastways, nothing worth hearing.'

'Monkey's paw?' said Mrs White curiously.

'Well, it's just a bit of what you might call magic, perhaps,' said the sergeant major offhandedly.

His three listeners leaned forward eagerly. The visitor absentmindedly put his empty glass to his lips and then set it down again. His host filled it for him.

'To look at,' said the sergeant major, fumbling in his pocket, 'it's just an ordinary little paw, dried to a mummy.'

He took something out of his pocket and proffered it. Mrs White drew back with a grimace, but her son, taking it, examined it curiously.

'And what is there special about it?' inquired Mr White, as he took it from his son, and having examined it, placed it upon the table.

'It had a spell put on it by an old fakir,' said the sergeant major, 'a very holy man. He wanted to show that fate ruled people's lives, and that those who interfered with it did so to their sorrow. He put a spell on it so that three separate men could each have three wishes from it.'

His manner was so impressive that his hearers were conscious that their light laughter jarred somewhat.

'Well, why don't you have three, sir?' said Herbert White cleverly.

The soldier regarded him in the way that middle age is wont to regard presumptuous youth. 'I have,' he said quietly, and his blotchy face whitened.

'And did you really have the three wishes granted?' asked Mrs White.

'I did,' said the sergeant major, and his glass tapped against his strong teeth.

'And has anybody else wished?' inquired the old lady.

'The first man had his three wishes, yes,' was the reply. 'I don't know what the first two were, but the third was for death. That's how I got the paw.'

His tones were so grave that a hush fell upon the group.

'If you've had your three wishes, it's no good to you now, then, Morris,' said the old man at last. 'What do you keep it for?'

The soldier shook his head. 'Fancy, I suppose,' he said slowly. 'I did have some idea of selling it, but I don't think I will. It has caused enough mischief already. Besides, people won't buy. They think it's a fairy tale, some of them, and those who do think anything of it want to try it first and pay me afterward.'

'If you could have another three wishes,' said the old man, eyeing him keenly, 'would you have them?'

'I don't know,' said the other. 'I don't know.'

He took the paw, and dangling it between his front finger and thumb, suddenly threw it upon the fire. White, with a slight cry, stooped down and snatched it off.

'Better let it burn,' said the soldier solemnly.

'If you don't want it, Morris,' said the old man, 'give it to me.'

'I won't,' said his friend doggedly. 'I threw it on the fire. If you keep it, don't blame me for what happens. Pitch it on the fire again, like a sensible man.'

The other shook his head and examined his new possession closely. 'How do you do it?' he inquired.

'Hold it up in your right hand and wish aloud,' said the sergeant major, 'but I warn you of the consequences.'

'Sounds like the Arabian Nights,' said Mrs White, as she rose and began to set the supper. 'Don't you think you might wish for four pairs of hands for me?'

Her husband drew the talisman from his pocket and then all three burst into laughter as the sergeant major, with a look of alarm on his face, caught him by the arm.

'If you must wish,' he said gruffly, 'wish for something sensible.'

Mr White dropped it back into his pocket, and placing chairs, motioned his friend to the table. In the business of supper the talisman was partly forgotten, and afterward the three sat listening in an enthralled fashion to a second instalment of the soldier's adventures in India.

'If the tale about the monkey's paw is not more truthful than those he has been telling us,' said Herbert, as the door closed behind their guest, just in time for him to catch the last train, 'we shan't make much out of it.'

'Did you give him anything for it, Father?' inquired Mrs White, regarding her husband closely.

'A trifle,' said he, colouring slightly. 'He didn't want it, but I made him take it. And he pressed me again to throw it away.'

'Likely,' said Herbert, with pretended horror. 'Why, we're going to be rich, and famous, and happy. Wish to be an emperor, Father, to begin with; then you can't be henpecked.'

He darted around the table, pursued by the maligned Mrs White armed with an antimacassar.

Mr White took the paw from his pocket and eyed it dubiously. 'I don't know what to wish for, and that's a fact,' he said slowly. 'It seems to me I've got all I want.'

'If you only cleared the house, you'd be quite happy, wouldn't you?' said Herbert, with his hand on his shoulder. 'Well, wish for two hundred pounds, then; that'll just do it.'

His father, smiling shamefacedly at his own credulity, held up the talisman, as his son, with a solemn face somewhat marred by a wink at his mother, sat down at the piano and struck a few impressive chords.

'I wish for two hundred pounds,' said the old man distinctly.

A fine crash from the piano greeted the words, interrupted by a shuddering cry from the old man. His wife and son ran toward him.

'It moved,' he cried, with a glance of disgust at the object as it lay on the floor. 'As I wished, it twisted in my hand like a snake.'

'Well, I don't see the money,' said his son, as he picked it up and placed it on the table, 'and I bet I never shall.'

'It must have been your fancy, Father,' said his wife, regarding him anxiously.

He shook his head. 'Never mind, though; there's no harm done, but it gave me a shock all the same.'

They sat down by the fire again while the two men finished their pipes. Outside, the wind was higher than ever, and the old man started nervously at the sound of a door banging upstairs. A silence unusual and depressing settled upon all three, which lasted until the old couple rose to retire for the night.

'I expect you'll find the cash tied up in a big bag in the middle of your bed,' said Herbert, as he bade them good night, 'and something horrible squatting up on top of the wardrobe watching you as you pocket your ill-gotten gains.'

In the brightness of the wintry sun next morning as it streamed over the breakfast table, Herbert laughed at his fears. There was an air of prosaic wholesomeness about the room which it had lacked on the previous night, and the dirty, shrivelled little paw was pitched on the sideboard with a carelessness which betokened no great belief in its virtues.

'I suppose all old soldiers are the same,' said Mrs White. 'The idea of our listening to such nonsense! How could wishes be granted in these days? And if they could, how could two hundred pounds hurt you, Father?'

'Might drop on his head from the sky,' said the frivolous Herbert.

'Morris said the things happened so naturally,' said his father, 'that you might, if you so wished, attribute it to coincidence.'

'Well, don't break into the money before I come back,' said Herbert, as he rose from the table. 'I'm afraid it'll turn you into a mean, avaricious man, and we shall have to disown you.'

His mother laughed, and following him to the door, watched him down the road, and returning to the breakfast table, was very happy at the expense of her husband's credulity. All of which did not prevent her from scurrying to the door at the postman's knock, nor prevent her from referring somewhat shortly to retired sergeant majors of bibulous habits, when she found that the post brought a tailor's bill.

'Herbert will have some more of his funny remarks, I expect, when he comes home,' she said, as they sat at dinner.

'I dare say,' said Mr White, pouring himself out some beer; 'but for all that, the thing moved in my hand; that I'll swear to.'

'You thought it did,' said the old lady soothingly.

'I say it did,' replied the other. 'There was no thought about it; I had just—What's the matter?'

His wife made no reply. She was watching the mysterious movements of a man outside, who, peering in an undecided fashion at the house, appeared to be trying to make up his mind to enter. In mental connection with the two hundred pounds, she noticed that the stranger was well dressed and wore a silk hat of glossy newness. Three times he paused at the gate, and then walked on again. The fourth time he stood with his hand upon it, and then with sudden resolution flung it open and walked up the path. Mrs White at the same moment placed her hands behind her, and hurriedly unfastening the strings of her apron, put that useful article of apparel beneath the cushion of her chair.

She brought the stranger, who seemed ill at ease, into the room. He gazed furtively at Mrs White, and listened in a preoccupied fashion as the old lady apologized for the appearance of the room, and her husband's coat, a garment which he usually reserved for the garden. She then waited as patiently as her sex would permit for him to broach his business, but he was at first strangely silent.

'I—was asked to call,' he said at last, and stooped and picked a piece of cotton from his trousers. 'I come from Maw and Meggins.'

The old lady started. 'Is anything the matter?' she asked breathlessly. 'Has anything happened to Herbert? What is it? What is it?'

Her husband interposed. 'There, there, Mother,' he said hastily. 'Sit down, and don't jump to conclusions. You've not brought bad news, I'm sure, sir,' and he eyed the other wistfully.

'I'm sorry—' began the visitor.

'Is he hurt?' demanded the mother.

The visitor bowed in assent. 'Badly hurt,' he said quietly, 'but he is not in any pain.'

'Oh, thank God!' said the old woman, clasping her hands. 'Thank God for that! Thank—'

She broke off suddenly as the sinister meaning of the assurance dawned upon her and she saw the awful confirmation of her fears in the other's averted face. She caught her breath, and turning to her slower-witted husband, laid her trembling old hand upon his. There was a long silence.

'He was caught in the machinery,' said the visitor at length, in a low voice.

'Caught in the machinery,' repeated Mr White, in a dazed fashion, 'yes.'

He sat staring blankly out at the window, and taking his wife's hand between his own, pressed it as he had been wont to do in their old courting days nearly forty years before.

'He was the only one left to us,' he said, turning gently to the visitor. 'It is hard.'

The other coughed, and rising, walked slowly to the window. 'The firm wished me to convey their sincere sympathy with you in your great loss,' he said, without looking around.

'I beg that you will understand I am only their servant and merely obeying orders.'

There was no reply; the old woman's face was white, her eyes staring, and her breath inaudible; on the husband's face was a look such as his friend the sergeant might have carried into his first action.

'I was to say that Maw and Meggins disclaim all responsibility,' continued the other. 'They admit no liability at all, but in consideration of your son's services they wish to present you with a certain sum as compensation.'

Mr White dropped his wife's hand, and rising to his feet, gazed with a look of horror at his visitor. His dry lips shaped the words, 'How much?'

'Two hundred pounds,' was the answer.

Unconscious of his wife's shriek, the old man smiled faintly, put out his hands like a sightless man, and dropped, a senseless heap, to the floor.

In the huge new cemetery, some two miles distant, the old people buried their dead, and came back to a house steeped in shadow and silence. It was all over so quickly that at first they could hardly realize it, and remained in a state of expectation, as though of something else to happen—something else which was to lighten this load, too heavy for old hearts to bear. But the days passed, and expectation gave place to resignation—the hopeless resignation of the old, sometimes miscalled apathy. Sometimes they hardly exchanged a word, for now they had nothing to talk about, and their days were long to weariness.

It was about a week after that that the old man, waking suddenly in the night, stretched out his hand and found himself alone. The room was in darkness, and the sound of subdued weeping came from the window. He raised himself in bed and listened.

'Come back,' he said tenderly. 'You will be cold.'

'It is colder for my son,' said the old woman, and wept afresh.

The sound of her sobs died away on his ears. The bed was warm, and his eyes heavy with sleep. He dozed fitfully, and then slept until a sudden cry from his wife awoke him with a start.

'The monkey's paw!' she cried wildly. 'The monkey's paw!'

He started up in alarm. 'Where? Where is it? What's the matter?' She came stumbling across the room toward him. 'I want it,' she said quietly. 'You've not destroyed it?'

'It's in the parlour, on the bracket,' he replied, marvelling. 'Why?'

She cried and laughed together, and bending over, kissed his cheek.

'I only just thought of it,' she said hysterically. 'Why didn't I think of it before? Why didn't you think of it?'

'Think of what?' he questioned.

'The other two wishes,' she replied rapidly. 'We've only had one.'

'Was not that enough?' he demanded fiercely.

'No,' she cried triumphantly; 'we'll have one more. Go down and get it quickly, and wish our boy alive again.'

The man sat up in bed and flung the bedclothes from his quaking limbs. 'Good God, you are mad!' he cried, aghast.

'Get it,' she panted; 'get it quickly, and wish—Oh, my boy, my boy!'

Her husband struck a match and lit the candle. 'Get back to bed,' he said unsteadily. 'You don't know what you are saying.'

'We had the first wish granted,' said the old woman feverishly; 'why not the second?'

'A coincidence,' stammered the old man.

'Go and get it and wish,' cried his wife, quivering with excitement.

The old man turned and regarded her, and his voice shook.

'He has been dead ten days, and besides he—I would not tell you else, but—I could only recognize him by his clothing. If he was too terrible for you to see then, how now?'

'Bring him back,' cried the old woman, and dragged him toward the door. 'Do you think I fear the child I have nursed?'

He went down in the darkness, and felt his way to the parlour, and then to the mantelpiece. The talisman was in its place, and a horrible fear that the unspoken wish might bring his mutilated son before him ere he could escape from the room seized upon him, and he caught his breath as he found that he had lost the direction of the door. His brow cold with sweat, he felt his way around the table, and groped along the wall until he found himself in the small passage with the unwholesome thing in his hand.

Even his wife's face seemed changed as he entered the room. It was white and expectant, and to his fears seemed to have an unnatural look upon it. He was afraid of her.

'Wish!' she cried, in a strong voice.

'It is foolish and wicked,' he faltered.

'Wish!' repeated his wife.

He raised his hand. 'I wish my son alive again.'

The talisman fell to the floor, and he regarded it shudderingly. Then he sank trembling into a chair as the old woman, with burning eyes, walked to the window and raised the blind.

He sat until he was chilled with the cold, glancing occasionally at the figure of the old woman peering through the window. The candle end, which had burned below the rim of the china candlestick, was throwing pulsating shadows on the ceiling and walls, until, with a flicker larger than the rest, it expired. The old man, with an unspeakable sense of relief at the failure of the talisman, crept back to his bed, and a minute or two afterward the old woman came silently and apathetically beside him.

Neither spoke, but both lay silently listening to the ticking of the clock. A stair creaked, and a squeaky mouse scurried noisily through the wall. The darkness was oppressive, and after lying for some time screwing up his courage, the husband took the box of matches, and striking one, went downstairs for a candle.

At the foot of the stairs the match went out, and he paused to strike another, and at the same moment a knock, so quiet and stealthy as to be scarcely audible, sounded on the front door.

The matches fell from his hand. He stood motionless, his breath suspended until the knock was repeated. Then he turned and fled swiftly back to his room, and closed the door behind him. A third knock sounded through the house.

'What's that?' cried the old woman, starting up.

'A rat,' said the old man, in shaking tones, 'a rat. It passed me on the stairs.'

His wife sat up in bed listening. A loud knock resounded through the house.

'It's Herbert!' she screamed. 'It's Herbert!'

She ran to the door, but her husband was before her, and catching her by the arm, held her tightly.

'What are you going to do?' he whispered hoarsely.

'It's my boy; it's Herbert!' she cried, struggling mechanically. 'I forgot it was two miles away. What are you holding me for? Let go. I must open the door.'

'For God's sake don't let it in,' cried the old man, trembling.

'You're afraid of your own son,' she cried, struggling. 'Let me go. I'm coming, Herbert; I'm coming.'

There was another knock, and another. The old woman with a sudden wrench broke free and ran from the room. Her husband followed to the landing, and called after her appealingly as she hurried downstairs. He heard the chain rattle back and the bottom bolt drawn slowly and stiffly from the socket. Then the old woman's voice, strained and panting.

'The bolt,' she cried loudly. 'Come down. I can't reach it.'

But her husband was on his hands and knees groping wildly on the floor in search of the paw. If he could only find it before the thing outside got in. A perfect fusillade of knocks reverberated through the house, and he heard the scraping of a chair as his wife put it down in the passage against the door. He heard the creaking of the bolt as it came slowly back, and at the same moment, he found the monkey's paw, and frantically breathed his third and last wish.

The knocking ceased suddenly, although the echoes of it were still in the house. He heard the chair drawn back and the door opened. A cold wind rushed up the staircase, and a long, loud wail of disappointment and misery from his wife gave him courage to run down to her side, and then to the gate beyond. The streetlamp flickering opposite shone on a quiet and deserted road.

2

THE LADY OF THE BARGE

The master of the barge Arabella sat in the stern of his craft with his right arm leaning on the tiller. A desultory conversation with the mate of a schooner, who was hanging over the side of his craft a few yards off, had come to a conclusion owing to a difference of opinion on the subject of religion. The skipper had argued so warmly that he almost fancied he must have inherited the tenets of the Seventh-day Baptists from his mother while the mate had surprised himself by the warmth of his advocacy of a form of Wesleyanism which would have made the members of that sect open their eyes with horror. He had, moreover, confirmed the skipper in the error of his ways by calling him a bargee, the ranks of the Baptists receiving a defender if not a recruit from that hour.

With the influence of the religious argument still upon him, the skipper, as the long summer's day gave place to night, fell to wondering where his own mate, who was also his brother-in-law, had got to. Lights which had been struggling with the twilight now burnt bright and strong, and the skipper, moving from the shadow to where a band of light fell across the deck, took out a worn silver watch and saw that it was ten o'clock.

Almost at the same moment a dark figure appeared on the jetty above and began to descend the ladder, and a strongly built young man of twenty-two sprang nimbly to the deck.

'Ten o'clock, Ted,' said the skipper, slowly. 'It'll be eleven in an hour's time,' said the mate, calmly.

'That'll do,' said the skipper, in a somewhat loud voice, as he noticed that his late adversary still occupied his favourite strained position, and a fortuitous expression of his mother's occurred to him: 'Don't talk to me; I've been arguing with a son of Belial for the last half-hour.'

'Bargee,' said the son of Belial, in a dispassionate voice.

'Don't take no notice of him, Ted,' said the skipper, pityingly.

'He wasn't talking to me,' said Ted. 'But never mind about him; I want to speak to you in private.'

'Fire away, my lad,' said the other, in a patronizing voice.

'Speak up,' said the voice from the schooner, encouragingly. 'I'm listening.'

There was no reply from the bargee. The master led the way to the cabin, and lighting a lamp, which appealed to more senses than one, took a seat on a locker, and again requested the other to fire away.

'Well, you see, it's this way,' began the mate, with a preliminary wriggle: 'there's a certain young woman—'

'A certain young what?' shouted the master of the Arabella.

'Woman,' repeated the mate, snappishly; 'you've heard of a woman afore, haven't you? Well, there's a certain young woman I'm walking out with I—'

'Walking out?' gasped the skipper. 'Why, I never 'eard o' such a thing.'

'You would ha' done if you'd been better looking, p'raps,' retorted the other. 'Well, I've offered this young woman to come for a trip with us.'

'Oh, you have, 'ave you!' said the skipper, sharply. 'And what do you think Louisa will say to it?'

'That's your look out,' said Louisa's brother, cheerfully. 'I'll make her up a bed for'ard, and we'll all be as happy as you please.'

He started suddenly. The mate of the schooner was indulging in a series of whistles of the most amatory description.

'There she is,' he said. 'I told her to wait outside.'

He ran upon deck, and his perturbed brother-in-law, following at his leisure, was just in time to see him descending the ladder with a young woman and a small handbag.

'This is my brother-in-law, Cap'n Gibbs,' said Ted, introducing the new arrival; 'smartest man at a barge on the river.'

The girl extended a neatly gloved hand, shook the skipper's affably, and looked wonderingly about her.

'It's very close to the water, Ted,' she said, dubiously.

The skipper coughed. 'We don't take passengers as a rule,' he said, awkwardly; 'we 'ain't got much convenience for them.'

'Never mind,' said the girl, kindly; 'I sha'nt expect too much.'

She turned away, and following the mate down to the cabin, went into ecstasies over the space-saving contrivances she found there. The drawers fitted in the skipper's bunk were a source of particular interest, and the owner watched with strong disapprobation through the skylight her efforts to make him an apple-pie bed with the limited means at her disposal. He went down below at once as a wet blanket.

'I was just shaking your bed up a bit,' said Miss Harris, reddening.

'I see you was,' said the skipper, briefly.

He tried to pluck up courage to tell her that he couldn't take her, but only succeeded in giving vent to an inhospitable cough.

'I'll get the supper,' said the mate, suddenly; 'you sit down, old man, and talk to Lucy.'

In honour of the visitor he spread a small cloth, and then proceeded to produce cold beef, pickles, and accessories in a manner which reminded Miss Harris of white rabbits from a conjurer's hat. Captain Gibbs, accepting the inevitable, ate his supper in silence and left them to their glances.

'We must make you up a bed, for'ard, Lucy,' said the mate, when they had finished.

Miss Harris started. 'Where's that?' she inquired.

'Other end o' the boat,' replied the mate, gathering up some bedding under his arm. 'You might bring a lantern, John.'

The skipper, who was feeling more sociable after a couple of glasses of beer, complied, and accompanied the couple to the tiny forecastle. A smell compounded of bilge, tar, paint, and other healthy disinfectants emerged as the scuttle was pushed back. The skipper dangled the lantern down and almost smiled.

'I can't sleep there,' said the girl, with decision. 'I shall die o' fright.'

'You'll get used to it,' said Ted, encouragingly, as he helped her down; 'it's quite dry and comfortable.'

He put his arm round her waist and squeezed her hand, and aided by this moral support, Miss Harris not only consented to remain, but found various advantages in the forecastle over the cabin, which had escaped the notice of previous voyagers.

'I'll leave you the lantern,' said the mate, making it fast, 'and we shall be on deck most o' the night. We get under way at two.'

He quitted the forecastle, followed by the skipper, after a polite but futile attempt to give him precedence, and made his way to the cabin for two or three hours' sleep.

'There'll be a row at the other end, Ted,' said the skipper, nervously, as he got into his bunk. 'Louisa's sure to blame me for letting you keep company with a gal like this. We was talking about you only the other day, and she said if you was married five years from now, it'ud be quite soon enough.'

'Let Loo mind her own business,' said the mate, sharply; 'she's not going to nag me. She's not my wife, thank goodness!'

He turned over and fell fast asleep, waking up fresh and bright three hours later, to commence what he fondly thought would be the pleasantest voyage of his life.

The Arabella dropped slowly down with the tide, the wind being so light that she was becalmed by every tall warehouse on the way. Off Greenwich, however, the breeze freshened somewhat, and a little later Miss Harris, looking somewhat pale as to complexion and untidy as to hair, came slowly on deck.

'Where's the looking-glass?' she asked, as Ted hastened to greet her. 'How does my hair look?'

'All wavy,' said the infatuated young man; 'all little curls and squiggles. Come down in the cabin; there's a glass there.'

Miss Harris, with a light nod to the skipper as he sat at the tiller, followed the mate below, and giving vent to a little cry of indignation as she saw herself in the glass, waved the amorous Ted on deck, and started work on her disarranged hair.

At breakfast-time a little friction was caused by what the mate bitterly termed the narrow-minded, old-fashioned ways of the skipper. He had arranged that the skipper should steer while he and Miss Harris breakfasted, but the coffee was no sooner on the table than the skipper called him, and relinquishing the helm in his favour, went below to do the honours. The mate protested.

'It's not proper,' said the skipper. 'Me and 'er will 'ave our meals together, and then you must have yours. She's under my care.'

Miss Harris assented blithely, and talk and laughter greeted the ears of the indignant mate as he steered. He went down at last to cold coffee and lukewarm herrings, returning to the deck after a hurried meal to find the skipper narrating some of his choicest experiences to an audience which hung on his lightest word.

The disregard they showed for his feelings was maddening, and for the first time in his life he became a prey to jealousy in its worst form. It was quite clear to him that the girl had become desperately enamoured of the skipper, and he racked his brain in a wild effort to discover the reason.

With an idea of reminding his brother-in-law of his position, he alluded two or three times in a casual fashion to his wife. The skipper hardly listened to him, and patting Miss Harris's cheek in a fatherly manner, regaled her with an anecdote of the mate's boyhood which the latter had spent a goodly portion of his life in denying. He denied it again, hotly, and Miss Harris, conquering for a time her laughter, reprimanded him severely for contradicting.

By the time dinner was ready he was in a state of sullen apathy, and when the meal was over and the couple came on deck again, so far forgot himself as to compliment Miss Harris upon her appetite.

'I'm ashamed of you, Ted,' said the skipper, with severity.

'I'm glad you know what shame is,' retorted the mate.

'If you can't be'ave yourself, you'd better keep a bit for'ard till you get in a better temper,' continued the skipper.

'I'll be pleased to,' said the smarting mate. 'I wish the barge was longer.'

'It couldn't be too long for me,' said Miss Harris, tossing her head.

'Be'aving like a schoolboy,' murmured the skipper.

'I know how to behave *my*-self,' said the mate, as he disappeared below. His head suddenly appeared again over the companion. 'If some people don't,' he added, and disappeared again.

He was pleased to notice as he ate his dinner that the giddy prattle above had ceased, and with his back turned toward the couple when he appeared on deck again, he lounged slowly forward until the skipper called him back again.

'Wot was them words you said just now, Ted?' he inquired.

The mate repeated them with gusto.

'Very good,' said the skipper, sharply; 'very good.'

'Don't you ever speak to me again,' said Miss Harris, with a stately air, 'because I won't answer you if you do.'

The mate displayed more of his schoolboy nature. 'Wait till you're spoken to,' he said, rudely. 'This is your gratefulness, I suppose?'

'Gratefulness?' said Miss Harris, with her chin in the air. 'What for?'

'For bringing you for a trip,' replied the mate, sternly.

'You bringing me for a trip!' said Miss Harris, scornfully. 'Captain Gibbs is the master here, I suppose. He is giving me the trip. You're only the mate.'

'Just so,' said the mate, with a grin at his brother-in-law, which made that worthy shift uneasily. 'I wonder what Loo will say when she sees you with a lady aboard?'

'She came to please you,' said Captain Gibbs, with haste.

'Ho! she did, did she?' jeered the mate. 'Prove it; only don't look to me to back you, that's all.'

The other eyed him in consternation, and his manner changed.

'Don't play the fool, Ted,' he said, not unkindly; 'you know what Loo is.'

'Well, I'm reckoning on that,' said the mate, deliberately. 'I'm going for'ard; don't let me interrupt you two. So long.'

He went slowly forward, and lighting his pipe, sprawled carelessly on the deck, and renounced the entire sex forthwith. At teatime the skipper attempted to reverse the procedure at the other meals; but as Miss Harris steadfastly declined to sit at the same table as the mate, his good intentions came to naught.

He made an appeal to what he termed the mate's better nature, after Miss Harris had retired to the seclusion of her bed-chamber, but in vain.

'She's nothing to do with me,' declared the mate, majestically. 'I wash my hands of her. She's a flirt. I'm like Louisa, I can't bear flirts.'

The skipper said no more, but his face was so worn that Miss Harris, when she came on deck in the early morning and found the barge gliding gently between the grassy banks of a river, attributed it to the difficulty of navigating so large a craft on so small and winding a stream.

'We shall be alongside in 'arf an hour,' said the skipper, eyeing her.

Miss Harris expressed her gratification.

'P'raps you wouldn't mind going down the fo'c'sle and staying there till we've made fast,' said the other. 'I'd take it as a favour. My owners don't like me to carry passengers.'

Miss Harris, who understood perfectly, said, 'Certainly,' and with a cold stare at the mate, who was at no pains to conceal his amusement, went below at once, thoughtfully closing the scuttle after her.

'There's no call to make mischief, Ted,' said the skipper, somewhat anxiously, as they swept round the last bend and came into view of Coalsham.

The mate said nothing, but stood by to take in sail as they ran swiftly toward the little quay. The pace slackened, and the Arabella, as though conscious of the contraband in her forecastle, crept slowly to where a stout, middle-aged woman, who bore a strong likeness to the mate, stood upon the quay.

'There's poor Loo,' said the mate, with a sigh.

The skipper made no reply to this infernal insinuation. The

barge ran alongside the quay and made fast.

'I thought you'd be up,' said Mrs Gibbs to her husband. 'Now come along to breakfast; Ted'll follow on.'

Captain Gibbs, dived down below for his coat, and slipping ashore, thankfully prepared to move off with his wife.

'Come on as soon as you can, Ted,' said the latter. 'Why, what on earth is he making that face for?'

She turned in amazement as her brother, making a pretence of catching her husband's eye, screwed his face up into a note of interrogation and gave a slight jerk with his thumb.

'Come along,' said Captain Gibbs, taking her arm with much affection.

'But what's Ted looking like that for?' demanded his wife, as she easily intercepted another choice facial expression of the mate's.

'Oh, it's his fun,' replied her husband, walking on.

'Fun?' repeated Mrs Gibbs, sharply. 'What's the matter, Ted.'

'Nothing,' replied the mate.

'Touch o' toothache,' said the skipper. 'Come along, Loo; I can just do with one o' your breakfasts.'

Mrs Gibbs suffered herself to be led on, and had got at least five yards on the way home, when she turned and looked back. The mate had still got the toothache, and was at that moment in all the agonies of a phenomenal twinge.

'There's something wrong here,' said Mrs Gibbs as she retraced her steps. 'Ted, what are you making that face for?'

'It's my own face,' said the mate, evasively.

Mrs Gibbs conceded the point, and added bitterly that it couldn't be helped. All the same she wanted to know what he meant by it.

'Ask John,' said the vindictive mate.

Mrs Gibbs asked. Her husband said he didn't know, and

added that Ted had been like it before, but he had not told her for fear of frightening her. Then he tried to induce her to go with him to the chemist's to get something for it.

Mrs Gibbs shook her head firmly, and boarding the barge, took a seat on the hatch and proceeded to catechise her brother as to his symptoms. He denied that there was anything the matter with him, while his eyes openly sought those of Captain Gibbs as though asking for instruction.

'You come home, Ted,' she said at length.

'I can't,' said the mate. 'I can't leave the ship.'

'Why not?' demanded his sister.

'Ask John,' said the mate again.

At this Mrs Gibbs's temper, which had been rising, gave way altogether, and she stamped fiercely upon the deck. A stamp of the foot has been for all time a rough-and-ready means of signalling; the fore-scuttle was drawn back, and the face of a young and pretty girl appeared framed in the opening. The mate raised his eyebrows with a helpless gesture, and as for the unfortunate skipper, any jury would have found him guilty without leaving the box. The wife of his bosom, with a flaming visage, turned and regarded him.

'You villain!' she said, in a choking voice.

Captain Gibbs caught his breath and looked appealingly at the mate.

'It's a little surprise for you, my dear,' he faltered, 'it's Ted's young lady.'

'Nothing of the kind,' said the mate, sharply.

'It's not? How dare you say such a thing?' demanded Miss Harris, stepping on to the deck.

'Well, you brought her aboard, Ted, you know you did,' pleaded the unhappy skipper.

The mate did not deny it, but his face was so full of grief and surprise that the other's heart sank within him.

'All right,' said the mate at last; 'have it your own way.'

'Hold your tongue, Ted,' shouted Mrs Gibbs; 'you're trying to shield him.'

'I tell you Ted brought her aboard, and they had a lover's quarrel,' said her unhappy spouse. 'It's nothing to do with me at all.'

'And that's why you told me Ted had got the toothache, and tried to get me off to the chemist's, I s'pose,' retorted his wife, with virulence. 'Do you think I'm a fool? How dare you ask a young woman on this barge? How dare you?'

'I didn't ask her,' said her husband.

'I s'pose she came without being asked,' sneered his wife, turning her regards to the passenger; 'she looks the sort that might. You brazen-faced girl!'

'Here, go easy, Loo,' interrupted the mate, flushing as he saw the girl's pale face.

'Mind your own business,' said his sister, violently.

'It is my business,' said the repentant mate. 'I brought her aboard, and then we quarrelled.'

'I've no doubt,' said his sister, bitterly; 'it's very pretty, but it won't do.'

'I swear it's the truth,' said the mate.

'Why did John keep it so quiet and hide her for, then?' demanded his sister.

'I came down for the trip,' said Miss Harris; 'that is all about it. There is nothing to make a fuss about. How much is it, Captain Gibbs?'

She produced a little purse from her pocket, but before the embarrassed skipper could reply, his infuriated wife struck it out of her hand. The mate sprang instinctively forward, but too late, and the purse fell with a splash into the water. The girl gave a faint cry and clasped her hands.

'How am I to get back?' she gasped.

'I'll see to that, Lucy,' said the mate. 'I'm very sorry—I've been a brute.'

'You?' said the indignant girl. 'I would sooner drown myself than be beholden to you.'

'I'm very sorry,' repeated the mate, humbly.

'There's enough of this play-acting,' interposed Mrs Gibbs. 'Get off this barge.'

'You stay where you are,' said the mate, authoritatively.

'Send that girl off this barge,' screamed Mrs Gibbs to her husband.

Captain Gibbs smiled in a silly fashion and scratched his head. 'Where is she to go?' he asked feebly.

'What does it matter to you where she goes?' cried his wife, fiercely. 'Send her off.'

The girl eyed her haughtily, and repulsing the mate as he strove to detain her, stepped to the side. Then she paused as he suddenly threw off his coat, and sitting down on the hatch, hastily removed his boots. The skipper, divining his intentions, seized him by the arm.

'Don't be a fool, Ted,' he gasped; 'you'll get under the barge.'

The mate shook him off, and went in with a splash which half drowned his adviser. Miss Harris, clasping her hands, ran to the side and gazed fearfully at the spot where he had disappeared, while his sister in a terrible voice seized the opportunity to point out to her husband the probably fatal results of his ill-doing. There was an anxious interval, and then the mate's head appeared above the water, and after a breathing-space disappeared again. The skipper, watching uneasily, stood by with a lifebelt.

'Come out, Ted,' screamed his sister as he came up for breath again.

The mate disappeared once more, but coming up for the

third time, hung on to the side of the barge to recover a bit. A clothed man in the water savours of disaster and looks alarming. Miss Harris began to cry.

'You'll be drowned,' she whimpered.

'Come out,' said Mrs Gibbs, in a raspy voice. She knelt on the deck and twined her fingers in his hair. The mate addressed her in terms rendered brotherly by pain.

'Never mind about the purse,' sobbed Miss Harris; 'it doesn't matter.'

'Will you make it up if I come out, then,' demanded the diver.

'No; I'll never speak to you again as long as I live,' said the girl, passionately.

The mate disappeared again. This time he was out of sight longer than usual, and when he came up merely tossed his arms weakly and went down again. There was a scream from the women, and a mighty splash as the skipper went overboard with a life-belt. The mate's head, black and shining, showed for a moment; the skipper grabbed him by the hair and towed him to the barge's side, and in the midst of a considerable hubbub both men were drawn from the water.

The skipper shook himself like a dog, but the mate lay on the deck inert in a puddle of water. Mrs Gibbs frantically slapped his hands; and Miss Harris, bending over him, rendered first aid by kissing him wildly.

Captain Gibbs pushed her away. 'He won't come round while you're a-kissing of him,' he cried, roughly.

To his indignant surprise the drowned man opened one eye and winked acquiescence. The skipper dropped his arms by his side and stared at him stupidly.

'I saw his eyelid twitch,' cried Mrs Gibbs, joyfully.

'He's all right,' said her indignant husband; ''e ain't born to be drowned, 'e ain't. I've spoilt a good suit of clothes for nothing.'

To his wife's amazement, he actually walked away from the insensible man, and with a boathook reached for his hat, which was floating by. Mrs Gibbs, still gazing in blank astonishment, caught a seraphic smile on the face of her brother as Miss Harris continued her ministrations, and in a pardonable fit of temper the overwrought woman gave him a box on the ear, which brought him round at once.

'Where am I?' he inquired, artlessly.

Mrs Gibbs told him. She also told him her opinion of him, and without plagiarizing her husband's words, came to the same conclusion as to his ultimate fate.

'You come along home with me,' she said, turning in a friendly fashion to the bewildered girl. 'They deserve what they've got—both of 'em. I only hope that they'll both get such awful colds that they won't find their voices for a twelvemonth.'

She took the girl by the arm and helped her ashore. They turned their heads once in the direction of the barge, and saw the justly incensed skipper keeping the mate's explanations and apologies at bay with a boat-hook. Then they went in to breakfast.

3

THE WELL

Two men stood in the billiard-room of an old country house, talking. Play, which had been of a half-hearted nature, was over, and they sat at the open window, looking out over the park stretching away beneath them, conversing idly.

'Your time's nearly up, Jem,' said one at length, 'this time six weeks you'll be yawning out the honeymoon and cursing the man—woman I mean—who invented them.' Jem Benson stretched his long limbs in the chair and grunted in dissent. 'I've never understood it,' continued Wilfred Carr, yawning. 'It's not in my line at all; I never had enough money for my own wants, let alone for two. Perhaps if I were as rich as you or Croesus I might regard it differently.'

There was just sufficient meaning in the latter part of the remark for his cousin to forbear to reply to it. He continued to gaze out of the window and to smoke slowly. 'Not being as rich as Croesus—or you,' resumed Carr, regarding him from beneath lowered lids, 'I paddle my own canoe down the stream of Time, and, tying it to my friends' door-posts, go in to eat their dinners.' 'Quite Venetian,' said Jem Benson, still looking out of the window. 'It's not a bad thing for you, Wilfred, that you have the door-posts and dinners—and friends.'

Carr grunted in his turn. 'Seriously though, Jem,' he said,

slowly, 'you're a lucky fellow, a very lucky fellow. If there is a better girl above ground than Olive, I should like to see her.'

'Yes,' said the other, quietly.

'She's such an exceptional girl,' continued Carr, staring out of the window. 'She's so good and gentle. She thinks you are a bundle of all the virtues.'

He laughed frankly and joyously, but the other man did not join him. 'Strong sense—of right and wrong, though,' continued Carr, musingly. 'Do you know, I believe that if she found out that you were not—'

'Not what?' demanded Benson, turning upon him fiercely, 'Not what?'

'Everything that you are,' returned his cousin, with a grin that belied his words, 'I believe she'd drop you.'

'Talk about something else,' said Benson, slowly; 'your pleasantries are not always in the best taste.'

Wilfred Carr rose and taking a cue from the rack, bent over the board and practiced one or two favourite shots. 'The only other subject I can talk about just at present is my own financial affairs,' he said slowly, as he walked round the table.

'Talk about something else,' said Benson again, bluntly.

'And the two things are connected,' said Carr, and dropping his cue he half sat on the table and eyed his cousin.

There was a long silence. Benson pitched the end of his cigar out of the window, and leaning back closed his eyes.

'Do you follow me?' inquired Carr at length.

Benson opened his eyes and nodded at the window.

'Do you want to follow my cigar?' he demanded.

'I should prefer to depart by the usual way for your sake,' returned the other, unabashed. 'If I left by the window all sorts of questions would be asked, and you know what a talkative chap I am.'

'So long as you don't talk about my affairs,' returned the

other, restraining himself by an obvious effort, 'you can talk yourself hoarse.'

'I'm in a mess,' said Carr, slowly, 'a devil of a mess. If I don't raise fifteen hundred by this day fortnight, I may be getting my board and lodging free.'

'Would that be any change?' questioned Benson.

'The quality would,' retorted the other. 'The address also would not be good. Seriously, Jem, will you let me have the fifteen hundred?'

'No,' said the other, simply.

Carr went white. 'It's to save me from ruin,' he said, thickly.

'I've helped you till I'm tired,' said Benson, turning and regarding him, 'and it is all to no good. If you've got into a mess, get out of it. You should not be so fond of giving autographs away.'

'It's foolish, I admit,' said Carr, deliberately. 'I won't do so any more. By the way, I've got some to sell. You needn't sneer. They're not my own.'

'Whose are they?' inquired the other.

'Yours.'

Benson got up from his chair and crossed over to him. 'What is this?' he asked, quietly. 'Blackmail?'

'Call it what you like,' said Carr. 'I've got some letters for sale, price fifteen hundred. And I know a man who would buy them at that price for the mere chance of getting Olive from you. I'll give you first offer.'

'If you have got any letters bearing my signature, you will be good enough to give them to me,' said Benson, very slowly.

'They're mine,' said Carr, lightly; 'given to me by the lady you wrote them to. I must say that they are not all in the best possible taste.'

His cousin reached forward suddenly, and catching him by the collar of his coat pinned him down on the table.

'Give me those letters,' he breathed, sticking his face close to Carr's.

'They're not here,' said Carr, struggling. 'I'm not a fool. Let me go, or I'll raise the price.'

The other man raised him from the table in his powerful hands, apparently with the intention of dashing his head against it. Then suddenly his hold relaxed as an astonished-looking maid-servant entered the room with letters. Carr sat up hastily.

'That's how it was done,' said Benson, for the girl's benefit as he took the letters.

'I don't wonder at the other man making him pay for it, then,' said Carr, blandly.

'You will give me those letters?' said Benson, suggestively, as the girl left the room.

'At the price I mentioned, yes,' said Carr; 'but so sure as I am a living man, if you lay your clumsy hands on me again, I'll double it. Now, I'll leave you for a time while you think it over.'

He took a cigar from the box and lighting it carefully quitted the room. His cousin waited until the door had closed behind him, and then turning to the window sat there in a fit of fury as silent as it was terrible.

The air was fresh and sweet from the park, heavy with the scent of new-mown grass. The fragrance of a cigar was now added to it, and glancing out he saw his cousin pacing slowly by. He rose and went to the door, and then, apparently altering his mind, he returned to the window and watched the figure of his cousin as it moved slowly away into the moonlight. Then he rose again, and, for a long time, the room was empty.

It was empty when Mrs Benson came in some time later to say good-night to her son on her way to bed. She walked slowly round the table, and pausing at the window gazed from it in idle thought, until she saw the figure of her son advancing with rapid strides toward the house. He looked up at the window.

'Good-night,' said she.

'Good-night,' said Benson, in a deep voice.

'Where is Wilfred?'

'Oh, he has gone,' said Benson.

'Gone?'

'We had a few words; he was wanting money again, and I gave him a piece of my mind. I don't think we shall see him again.'

'Poor Wilfred!' sighed Mrs Benson. 'He is always in trouble of some sort. I hope that you were not too hard upon him.'

'No more than he deserved,' said her son, sternly. 'Good night.'

The well, which had long ago fallen into disuse, was almost hidden by the thick tangle of undergrowth which ran riot at that corner of the old park. It was partly covered by the shrunken half of a lid, above which a rusty windlass creaked in company with the music of the pines when the wind blew strongly. The full light of the sun never reached it, and the ground surrounding it was moist and green when other parts of the park were gaping with the heat.

Two people walking slowly round the park in the fragrant stillness of a summer evening strayed in the direction of the well.

'No use going through this wilderness, Olive,' said Benson, pausing on the outskirts of the pines and eyeing with some disfavour the gloom beyond.

'Best part of the park,' said the girl briskly; 'you know it's my favourite spot.'

'I know you're very fond of sitting on the coping,' said the man slowly, 'and I wish you wouldn't. One day you will lean back too far and fall in.'

'And make the acquaintance of Truth,' said Olive lightly. 'Come along.'

She ran from him and was lost in the shadow of the pines, the bracken crackling beneath her feet as she ran. Her companion followed slowly, and emerging from the gloom saw her poised daintily on the edge of the well with her feet hidden in the rank grass and nettles which surrounded it. She motioned her companion to take a seat by her side, and smiled softly as she felt a strong arm passed about her waist.

'I like this place,' said she, breaking a long silence, 'it is so dismal —so uncanny. Do you know I wouldn't dare to sit here alone, Jem. I should imagine that all sorts of dreadful things were hidden behind the bushes and trees, waiting to spring out on me. Ugh!'

'You'd better let me take you in,' said her companion tenderly; 'the well isn't always wholesome, especially in the hot weather.

'Let's make a move.'

The girl gave an obstinate little shake, and settled herself more securely on her seat.

'Smoke your cigar in peace,' she said quietly. 'I am settled here for a quiet talk. Has anything been heard of Wilfred yet?'

'Nothing.'

'Quite a dramatic disappearance, isn't it?' she continued. 'Another scrape, I suppose, and another letter for you in the same old strain; "Dear Jem, help me out."'

Jem Benson blew a cloud of fragrant smoke into the air, and holding his cigar between his teeth brushed away the ash from his coat sleeves.

'I wonder what he would have done without you,' said the girl, pressing his arm affectionately. 'Gone under long ago, I suppose. When we are married, Jem, I shall presume upon the relationship to lecture him. He is very wild, but he has his good points, poor fellow.'

'I never saw them,' said Benson, with startling bitterness.

'God knows I never saw them.'

'He is nobody's enemy but his own,' said the girl, startled by this outburst.

'You don't know much about him,' said the other, sharply. 'He was not above blackmail; not above ruining the life of a friend to do himself a benefit. A loafer, a cur, and a liar!'

The girl looked up at him soberly but timidly and took his arm without a word, and they both sat silent while evening deepened into night and the beams of the moon, filtering through the branches, surrounded them with a silver network. Her head sank upon his shoulder, till suddenly with a sharp cry she sprang to her feet.

'What was that?' she cried breathlessly.

'What was what?' demanded Benson, springing up and clutching her fast by the arm.

She caught her breath and tried to laugh.

'You're hurting me, Jem.'

His hold relaxed.

'What is the matter?' he asked gently.

'What was it startled you?'

'I was startled,' she said, slowly, putting her hands on his shoulder. 'I suppose the words I used just now are ringing in my ears, but I fancied that somebody behind us whispered, "Jem, help me out."'

'Fancy,' repeated Benson, and his voice shook; 'but these fancies are not good for you. You—are frightened—at the dark and the gloom of these trees. Let me take you back to the house.'

'No, I'm not frightened,' said the girl, reseating herself. 'I should never be really frightened of anything when you were with me, Jem. I'm surprised at myself for being so silly.'

The man made no reply but stood, a strong, dark figure, a yard or two from the well, as though waiting for her to join him.

'Come and sit down, sir,' cried Olive, patting the brickwork with her small, white hand, 'one would think that you did not like your company.'

He obeyed slowly and took a seat by her side, drawing so hard at his cigar that the light of it shone upon his fare at every breath. He passed his arm, firm and rigid as steel, behind her, with his hand resting on the brickwork beyond.

'Are you warm enough?' he asked tenderly, as she made a little movement. 'Pretty fair,' she shivered; 'one oughtn't to be cold at this time of the year, but there's a cold, damp air comes up from the well.'

As she spoke a faint splash sounded from the depths below, and for the second time that evening, she sprang from the well with a little cry of dismay.

'What is it now?' he asked in a fearful voice. He stood by her side and gazed at the well, as though half expecting to see the cause of her alarm emerge from it.

'Oh, my bracelet,' she cried in distress, 'my poor mother's bracelet. I've dropped it down the well.'

'Your bracelet!' repeated Benson, dully. 'Your bracelet? The diamond one?'

'The one that was my mother's,' said Olive. 'Oh, we can get it back surely. We must have the water drained off.'

'Your bracelet!' repeated Benson, stupidly.

'Jem,' said the girl in terrified tones, 'dear Jem, what is the matter?'

For the man she loved was standing regarding her with horror. The moon which touched it was not responsible for all the whiteness of the distorted face, and she shrank back in fear to the edge of the well. He saw her fear and by a mighty effort regained his composure and took her hand.

'Poor little girl,' he murmured, 'you frightened me. I was not looking when you cried, and I thought that you were slipping from my arms, down—down—'

His voice broke, and the girl throwing herself into his arms clung to him convulsively.

'There, there,' said Benson, fondly, 'don't cry, don't cry.'

'To-morrow,' said Olive, half-laughing, half-crying, 'we will all come round the well with hook and line and fish for it. It will be quite a new sport.'

'No, we must try some other way,' said Benson. 'You shall have it back.'

'How?' asked the girl.

'You shall see,' said Benson. 'To-morrow morning at latest you shall have it back. Till then promise me that you will not mention your loss to anyone. Promise.'

'I promise,' said Olive, wonderingly. 'But why not?'

'It is of great value, for one thing, and—But there—there are many reasons. For one thing it is my duty to get it for you.'

'Wouldn't you like to jump down for it?' she asked mischievously. 'Listen.'

She stooped for a stone and dropped it down.

'Fancy being where that is now,' she said, peering into the blackness; 'fancy going round and round like a mouse in a pail, clutching at the slimy sides, with the water filling your mouth, and looking up to the little patch of sky above.'

'You had better come in,' said Benson, very quietly. 'You are developing a taste for the morbid and horrible.'

The girl turned, and taking his arm walked slowly in the direction of the house; Mrs Benson, who was sitting in the porch, rose to receive them.

'You shouldn't have kept her out so long,' she said chidingly. 'Where have you been?'

'Sitting on the well,' said Olive, smiling, 'discussing our future.'

'I don't believe that place is healthy,' said Mrs Benson,

emphatically. 'I really think it might be filled in, Jem.'

'All right,' said her son, slowly. 'Pity it wasn't filled in long ago.'

He took the chair vacated by his mother as she entered the house with Olive, and with his hands hanging limply over the sides sat in deep thought. After a time he rose, and going upstairs to a room which was set apart for sporting requisites selected a sea fishing line and some hooks and stole softly downstairs again. He walked swiftly across the park in the direction of the well, turning before he entered the shadow of the trees to look back at the lighted windows of the house. Then having arranged his line he sat on the edge of the well and cautiously lowered it.

He sat with his lips compressed, occasionally looking about him in a startled fashion, as though he half expected to see something peering at him from the belt of trees. Time after time he lowered his line until at length in pulling it up he heard a little metallic tinkle against the side of the well.

He held his breath then, and forgetting his fears drew the line in inch by inch, so as not to lose its precious burden. His pulse beat rapidly, and his eyes were bright. As the line came slowly in he saw the catch hanging to the hook, and with a steady hand drew the last few feet in. Then he saw that instead of the bracelet he had hooked a bunch of keys.

With a faint cry he shook them from the hook into the water below, and stood breathing heavily. Not a sound broke the stillness of the night. He walked up and down a bit and stretched his great muscles; then he came back to the well and resumed his task.

For an hour or more the line was lowered without result. In his eagerness he forgot his fears, and with eyes bent down the well fished slowly and carefully. Twice the hook became entangled in something, and was with difficulty released. It caught a third time, and all his efforts failed to free it. Then he dropped the line down the well, and with head bent walked toward the house.

He went first to the stables at the rear, and then retiring to his room for some time paced restlessly up and down. Then without removing his clothes he flung himself upon the bed and fell into a troubled sleep.

Long before anybody else was astir he arose and stole softly downstairs. The sunlight was stealing in at every crevice, and flashing in long streaks across the darkened rooms. The dining-room into which he looked struck chill and cheerless in the dark yellow light which came through the lowered blinds. He remembered that it had the same appearance when his father lay dead in the house; now, as then, everything seemed ghastly and unreal; the very chairs standing as their occupants had left them the night before seemed to be indulging in some dark communication of ideas.

Slowly and noiselessly he opened the hall door and passed into the fragrant air beyond. The sun was shining on the drenched grass and trees, and a slowly vanishing white mist rolled like smoke about the grounds. For a moment he stood, breathing deeply the sweet air of the morning, and then walked slowly in the direction of the stables.

The rusty creaking of a pump-handle and a spatter of water upon the red-tiled courtyard showed that somebody else was astir, and a few steps farther he beheld a brawny, sandy-haired man gasping wildly under severe self-infliction at the pump.

'Everything ready, George?' he asked quietly.

'Yes, sir,' said the man, straightening up suddenly and touching his forehead. 'Bob's just finishing the arrangements inside. It's a lovely morning for a dip. The water in that well must be just icy.'

'Be as quick as you can,' said Benson, impatiently.

'Very good, sir,' said George, burnishing his face harshly with a very small towel which had been hanging over the top of the pump. 'Hurry up, Bob.'

In answer to his summons a man appeared at the door of the stable with a coil of stout rope over his arm and a large metal candlestick in his hand.

'Just to try the air, sir,' said George, following his master's glance, 'a well gets rather foul sometimes, but if a candle can live down it, a man can.'

His master nodded, and the man, hastily pulling up the neck of his shirt and thrusting his arms into his coat, followed him as he led the way slowly to the well.

'Beg pardon, sir,' said George, drawing up to his side, 'but you are not looking over and above well this morning. If you'll let me go down I'd enjoy the bath.'

'No, no,' said Benson, peremptorily.

'You ain't fit to go down, sir,' persisted his follower. 'I've never seen you look so before. Now if—'

'Mind your business,' said his master curtly.

George became silent and the three walked with swinging strides through the long wet grass to the well. Bob flung the rope on the ground and at a sign from his master handed him the candlestick.

'Here's the line for it, sir,' said Bob, fumbling in his pockets.

Benson took it from him and slowly tied it to the candlestick. Then he placed it on the edge of the well, and striking a match, lit the candle and began slowly to lower it.

'Hold hard, sir,' said George, quickly, laying his hand on his arm, 'you must tilt it or the string'll burn through.'

Even as he spoke the string parted and the candlestick fell into the water below.

Benson swore quietly.

'I'll soon get another,' said George, starting up.

'Never mind, the well's all right,' said Benson.

'It won't take a moment, sir,' said the other over his shoulder.

'Are you master here, or am I?' said Benson hoarsely.

George came back slowly, a glance at his master's face stopping the protest upon his tongue, and he stood by watching him sulkily as he sat on the well and removed his outer garments. Both men watched him curiously, as having completed his preparations he stood grim and silent with his hands by his sides.

'I wish you'd let me go, sir,' said George, plucking up courage to address him. 'You ain't fit to go, you've got a chill or something. I shouldn't wonder it's the typhoid. They've got it in the village bad.'

For a moment Benson looked at him angrily, then his gaze softened. 'Not this time, George,' he said, quietly. He took the looped end of the rope and placed it under his arms, and sitting down threw one leg over the side of the well.

'How are you going about it, sir?' queried George, laying hold of the rope and signing to Bob to do the same.

'I'll call out when I reach the water,' said Benson; 'then pay out three yards more quickly so that I can get to the bottom.'

'Very good, sir,' answered both.

Their master threw the other leg over the coping and sat motionless. His back was turned toward the men as he sat with head bent, looking down the shaft. He sat for so long that George became uneasy.

'All right, sir?' he inquired.

'Yes,' said Benson, slowly. 'If I tug at the rope, George, pull up at once. Lower away.'

The rope passed steadily through their hands until a hollow cry from the darkness below and a faint splashing warned them that he had reached the water. They gave him three yards more and stood with relaxed grasp and strained ears, waiting.

'He's gone under,' said Bob in a low voice.

The other nodded, and moistening his huge palms took a firmer grip of the rope.

Fully a minute passed, and the men began to exchange uneasy glances. Then a sudden tremendous jerk followed by a series of feebler ones nearly tore the rope from their grasp.

'Pull!' shouted George, placing one foot on the side and hauling desperately. 'Pull! pull! He's stuck fast; he's not coming; PULL!'

In response to their terrific exertions the rope came slowly in, inch by inch, until at length a violent splashing was heard, and at the same moment a scream of unutterable horror came echoing up the shaft.

'What a weight he is!' panted Bob. 'He's stuck fast or something. Keep still, sir; for heaven's sake, keep still.'

For the taut rope was being jerked violently by the struggles of the weight at the end of it. Both men with grunts and sighs hauled it in foot by foot.

'All right, sir,' cried George, cheerfully.

He had one foot against the well, and was pulling manfully; the burden was nearing the top. A long pull and a strong pull, and the face of a dead man with mud in the eyes and nostrils came peering over the edge. Behind it was the ghastly face of his master; but this he saw too late, for with a great cry he let go his hold of the rope and stepped back. The suddenness overthrew his assistant, and the rope tore through his hands. There was a frightful splash.

'You fool!' stammered Bob, and ran to the well helplessly.

'Run!' cried George. 'Run for another line.'

He bent over the coping and called eagerly down as his assistant sped back to the stables shouting wildly. His voice re-echoed down the shaft, but all else was silence.

4

THE TOLL-HOUSE

'IT'S all nonsense,' said Jack Barnes. 'Of course people have died in the house; people die in every house. As for the noises—wind in the chimney and rats in the wainscot are very convincing to a nervous man. Give me another cup of tea, Meagle.'

'Lester and White are first,' said Meagle, who was presiding at the tea-table of the Three Feathers Inn. 'You've had two.'

Lester and White finished their cups with irritating slowness, pausing between sips to sniff the aroma, and to discover the sex and dates of arrival of the 'strangers' which floated in some numbers in the beverage. Mr Meagle served them to the brim, and then, turning to the grimly expectant Mr Barnes, blandly requested him to ring for hot water.

'We'll try and keep your nerves in their present healthy condition,' he remarked. 'For my part I have a sort of half-and-half belief in the supernatural.'

'All sensible people have,' said Lester. 'An aunt of mine saw a ghost once.'

White nodded.

'I had an uncle that saw one,' he said.

'It always is somebody else that sees them,' said Barnes.

'Well, there is the house,' said Meagle, 'a large house at an absurdly low rent, and nobody will take it. It has taken toll of at least one life of every family that has lived there—however short the time—and since it has stood empty caretaker after caretaker has died there. The last caretaker died fifteen years ago.'

'Exactly,' said Barnes. 'Long enough ago for legends to accumulate.'

'I'll bet you a sovereign you won't spend the night there alone, for all your talk,' said White suddenly.

'And I,' said Lester.

'No,' said Barnes slowly. 'I don't believe in ghosts nor in any supernatural things whatever; all the same, I admit that I should not care to pass a night there alone.'

'But why not?' inquired White.

'Wind in the chimney,' said Meagle, with a grin.

'Rats in the wainscot,' chimed in Lester.

'As you like,' said Barnes, colouring.

'Suppose we all go?' said Meagle. 'Start after supper, and get there about eleven? We have been walking for ten days now without an adventure—except Barnes's discovery that ditch-water smells longest. It will be a novelty, at any rate, and, if we break the spell by all surviving, the grateful owner ought to come down handsome.'

'Let's see what the landlord has to say about it first,' said Lester. 'There is no fun in passing a night in an ordinary empty house. Let us make sure that it is haunted.'

He rang the bell, and, sending for the landlord, appealed to him in the name of our common humanity not to let them waste a night watching in a house in which spectres and hobgoblins had no part. The reply was more than reassuring, and the landlord, after describing with considerable art the exact appearance of a head which had been seen hanging out of a window in the moonlight, wound up with a polite but urgent request that they would settle his bill before they went.

'It's all very well for you young gentlemen to have your fun,' he said indulgently; 'but, supposing as how you are all found dead in the morning, what about me? It ain't called the Toll-House for nothing, you know.'

'Who died there last?' inquired Barnes, with an air of polite derision.

'A tramp,' was the reply. 'He went there for the sake of half-a-crown, and they found him next morning hanging from the balusters, dead.'

'Suicide,' said Barnes. 'Unsound mind.'

The landlord nodded. 'That's what the jury brought it in,' he said slowly; 'but his mind was sound enough when he went in there. I'd known him, off and on, for years. I'm a poor man, but I wouldn't spend the night in that house for a hundred pounds.'

He repeated this remark as they started on their expedition a few hours later. They left as the inn was closing for the night; bolts shot noisily behind them, and, as the regular customers trudged slowly homewards, they set off at a brisk pace in the direction of the house. Most of the cottages were already in darkness, and lights in others went out as they passed.

'It seems rather hard that we have got to lose a night's rest in order to convince Barnes of the existence of ghosts,' said White.

'It's in a good cause,' said Meagle. 'A most worthy object; and something seems to tell me that we shall succeed. You didn't forget the candles, Lester?'

'I have brought two,' was the reply; 'all the old man could spare.'

There was but little moon, and the night was cloudy. The road between high hedges was dark, and in one place, where it ran through a wood, so black that they twice stumbled in the uneven ground at the side of it.

'Fancy leaving our comfortable beds for this!' said White again. 'Let me see; this desirable residential sepulchre lies to the right, doesn't it?'

'Farther on,' said Meagle.

They walked on for some time in silence, broken only by White's tribute to the softness, the cleanliness, and the comfort of the bed which was receding farther and farther into the distance. Under Meagle's guidance they turned off at last to the right, and, after a walk of a quarter of a mile, saw the gates of the house before them.

The lodge was almost hidden by overgrown shrubs and the drive was choked with rank growths. Meagle leading, they pushed through it until the dark pile of the house loomed above them.

'There is a window at the back where we can get in, so the landlord says,' said Lester, as they stood before the hall door.

'Window?' said Meagle. 'Nonsense. Let's do the thing properly. Where's the knocker?'

He felt for it in the darkness and gave a thundering rat-tat-tat at the door.

'Don't play the fool,' said Barnes crossly.

'Ghostly servants are all asleep,' said Meagle gravely, 'but I'll wake them up before I've done with them. It's scandalous keeping us out here in the dark.'

He plied the knocker again, and the noise volleyed in the emptiness beyond. Then with a sudden exclamation he put out his hands and stumbled forward.

'Why, it was open all the time,' he said, with an odd catch in his voice. 'Come on.'

'I don't believe it was open,' said Lester, hanging back. 'Somebody is playing us a trick.'

'Nonsense,' said Meagle sharply. 'Give me a candle. Thanks.

Who's got a match?'

Barnes produced a box and struck one, and Meagle, shielding the candle with his hand, led the way forward to the foot of the stairs. 'Shut the door, somebody,' he said; 'there's too much draught.'

'It is shut,' said White, glancing behind him.

Meagle fingered his chin. 'Who shut it?' he inquired, looking from one to the other. 'Who came in last?'

'I did,' said Lester, 'but I don't remember shutting it—perhaps I did, though.'

Meagle, about to speak, thought better of it, and, still carefully guarding the flame, began to explore the house, with the others close behind. Shadows danced on the walls and lurked in the corners as they proceeded. At the end of the passage they found a second staircase, and ascending it slowly gained the first floor.

'Careful!' said Meagle, as they gained the landing.

He held the candle forward and showed where the balusters had broken away. Then he peered curiously into the void beneath.

'This is where the tramp hanged himself, I suppose,' he said thoughtfully.

'You've got an unwholesome mind,' said White, as they walked on. 'This place is quite creepy enough without you remembering that. Now let's find a comfortable room and have a little nip of whisky apiece and a pipe. How will this do?'

He opened a door at the end of the passage and revealed a small square room. Meagle led the way with the candle, and, first melting a drop or two of tallow, stuck it on the mantelpiece. The others seated themselves on the floor and watched pleasantly as White drew from his pocket a small bottle of whisky and a tin cup.

'H'm! I've forgotten the water,' he exclaimed.

'I'll soon get some,' said Meagle.

He tugged violently at the bell-handle, and the rusty jangling of a bell sounded from a distant kitchen. He rang again.

'Don't play the fool,' said Barnes roughly.

Meagle laughed. 'I only wanted to convince you,' he said kindly. 'There ought to be, at any rate, one ghost in the servants' hall.'

Barnes held up his hand for silence.

'Yes?' said Meagle, with a grin at the other two. 'Is anybody coming?'

'Suppose we drop this game and go back,' said Barnes suddenly. 'I don't believe in spirits, but nerves are outside anybody's command. You may laugh as you like, but it really seemed to me that I heard a door open below and steps on the stairs.'

His voice was drowned in a roar of laughter.

'He is coming round,' said Meagle, with a smirk. 'By the time I have done with him he will be a confirmed believer. Well, who will go and get some water? Will, you, Barnes?'

'No,' was the reply.

'If there is any it might not be safe to drink after all these years,' said Lester. 'We must do without it.'

Meagle nodded, and taking a seat on the floor held out his hand for the cup. Pipes were lit, and the clean, wholesome smell of tobacco filled the room. White produced a pack of cards; talk and laughter rang through the room and died away reluctantly in distant corridors.

'Empty rooms always delude me into the belief that I possess a deep voice,' said Meagle. 'To-morrow I—'

He started up with a smothered exclamation as the light went out suddenly and something struck him on the head. The others sprang to their feet. Then Meagle laughed.

'It's the candle,' he exclaimed. 'I didn't stick it enough.'

Barnes struck a match, and re-lighting the candle, stuck it on the mantelpiece, and sitting down took up his cards again.

'What was I going to say?' said Meagle. 'Oh, I know; to-morrow I—'

'Listen!' said White, laying his hand on the other's sleeve. 'Upon my word I really thought I heard a laugh.'

'Look here!' said Barnes. 'What do you say to going back? I've had enough of this. I keep fancying that I hear things too; sounds of something moving about in the passage outside. I know it's only fancy, but it's uncomfortable.'

'You go if you want to,' said Meagle, 'and we will play dummy. Or you might ask the tramp to take your hand for you, as you go downstairs.'

Barnes shivered and exclaimed angrily. He got up, and, walking to the half-closed door, listened.

'Go outside,' said Meagle, winking at the other two. 'I'll dare you to go down to the hall door and back by yourself.'

Barnes came back, and, bending forward, lit his pipe at the candle.

'I am nervous, but rational,' he said, blowing out a thin cloud of smoke. 'My nerves tell me that there is something prowling up and down the long passage outside; my reason tells me that that is all nonsense. Where are my cards?'

He sat down again, and, taking up his hand, looked through it carefully and led.

'Your play, White,' he said, after a pause.

White made no sign.

'Why, he is asleep,' said Meagle. 'Wake up, old man. Wake up and play.'

Lester, who was sitting next to him, took the sleeping man by the arm and shook him, gently at first and then with some roughness but White, with his back against the wall and his head bowed, made no sign. Meagle bawled in his ear, and then turned a puzzled face to the others.

'He sleeps like the dead,' he said, grimacing. 'Well, there are still three of us to keep each other company.'

'Yes,' said Lester, nodding. 'Unless—Good Lord! suppose—'

He broke off, and eyed them, trembling.

'Suppose what?' inquired Meagle.

'Nothing,' stammered Lester. 'Let's wake him. Try him again. White! WHITE!'

'It's no good,' said Meagle seriously; 'there's something wrong about that sleep.'

'That's what I meant,' said Lester; 'and if he goes to sleep like that, why shouldn't—'

Meagle sprang to his feet. 'Nonsense,' he said roughly. 'He's tired out; that's all. Still, let's take him up and clear out. You take his legs and Barnes will lead the way with the candle. Yes? Who's that?'

He looked up quickly towards the door. 'Thought I heard somebody tap,' he said, with a shamefaced laugh. 'Now, Lester, up with him. One, two—Lester! Lester!'

He sprang forward too late; Lester, with his face buried in his arms, had rolled over on the floor fast asleep, and his utmost efforts failed to awake him.

'He—is—asleep,' he stammered. 'Asleep!'

Barnes, who had taken the candle from the mantelpiece, stood peering at the sleepers in silence and dropping tallow over the floor.

'We must get out of this,' said Meagle. 'Quick!'

Barnes hesitated. 'We can't leave them here—' he began.

'We must,' said Meagle, in strident tones. 'If you go to sleep I shall go—Quick! Come!'

He seized the other by the arm and strove to drag him to the door. Barnes shook him off, and, putting the candle back on the mantelpiece, tried again to arouse the sleepers.

'It's no good,' he said at last, and, turning from them, watched Meagle. 'Don't you go to sleep,' he said anxiously.

Meagle shook his head, and they stood for some time in uneasy silence. 'May as well shut the door,' said Barnes at last.

He crossed over and closed it gently. Then at a scuffling noise behind him he turned and saw Meagle in a heap on the hearthstone.

With a sharp catch in his breath he stood motionless. Inside the room the candle, fluttering in the draught, showed dimly the grotesque attitudes of the sleepers. Beyond the door there seemed to his overwrought imagination a strange and stealthy unrest. He tried to whistle, but his lips were parched, and in a mechanical fashion he stooped, and began to pick up the cards which littered the floor.

He stopped once or twice and stood with bent head listening. The unrest outside seemed to increase; a loud creaking sounded from the stairs.

'Who is there?' he cried loudly.

The creaking ceased. He crossed to the door, and, flinging it open, strode out into the corridor. As he walked his fears left him suddenly.

'Come on!' he cried, with a low laugh. 'All of you! All of you! Show your faces—your infernal ugly faces! Don't skulk!'

He laughed again and walked on; and the heap in the fireplace put out its head tortoise fashion and listened in horror to the retreating footsteps. Not until they had become inaudible in the distance did the listeners' features relax.

'Good Lord, Lester, we've driven him mad,' he said, in a frightened whisper. 'We must go after him.'

There was no reply. Meagle sprang to his feet.

'Do you hear?' he cried. 'Stop your fooling now; this is serious. White! Lester! Do you hear?'

He bent and surveyed them in angry bewilderment. 'All

right,' he said, in a trembling voice. 'You won't frighten me, you know.'

He turned away and walked with exaggerated carelessness in the direction of the door. He even went outside and peeped through the crack, but the sleepers did not stir. He glanced into the blackness behind, and then came hastily into the room again.

He stood for a few seconds regarding them. The stillness in the house was horrible; he could not even hear them breathe. With a sudden resolution he snatched the candle from the mantelpiece and held the flame to White's finger. Then as he reeled back stupefied, the footsteps again became audible.

He stood with the candle in his shaking hand, listening. He heard them ascending the farther staircase, but they stopped suddenly as he went to the door. He walked a little way along the passage, and they went scurrying down the stairs and then at a jog-trot along the corridor below. He went back to the main staircase, and they ceased again.

For a time he hung over the balusters, listening and trying to pierce the blackness below; then slowly, step by step, he made his way downstairs, and, holding the candle above his head, peered about him.

'Barnes!' he called. 'Where are you?'

Shaking with fright, he made his way along the passage, and summoning up all his courage, pushed open doors and gazed fearfully into empty rooms. Then, quite suddenly, he heard the footsteps in front of him.

He followed slowly for fear of extinguishing the candle, until they led him at last into a vast bare kitchen, with damp walls and a broken floor. In front of him a door leading into an inside room had just closed. He ran towards it and flung it open, and a cold air blew out the candle. He stood aghast.

'Barnes!' he cried again. 'Don't be afraid! It is I—Meagle!'

There was no answer. He stood gazing into the darkness, and all the time the idea of something close at hand watching was upon him. Then suddenly the steps broke out overhead again.

He drew back hastily, and passing through the kitchen groped his way along the narrow passages. He could now see better in the darkness, and finding himself at last at the foot of the staircase, began to ascend it noiselessly. He reached the landing just in time to see a figure disappear round the angle of a wall. Still careful to make no noise, he followed the sound of the steps until they led him to the top floor, and he cornered the chase at the end of a short passage.

'Barnes!' he whispered. 'Barnes!'

Something stirred in the darkness. A small circular window at the end of the passage just softened the blackness and revealed the dim outlines of a motionless figure. Meagle, in place of advancing, stood almost as still as a sudden horrible doubt took possession of him. With his eyes fixed on the shape in front he fell back slowly, and, as it advanced upon him, burst into a terrible cry.

'Barnes! For God's sake! Is it you?'

The echoes of his voice left the air quivering, but the figure before him paid no heed. For a moment he tried to brace his courage up to endure its approach, then with a smothered cry he turned and fled.

The passages wound like a maze, and he threaded them blindly in a vain search for the stairs. If he could get down and open the hall door——

He caught his breath in a sob; the steps had begun again. At a lumbering trot they clattered up and down the bare passages, in and out, up and down, as though in search of him. He stood appalled, and then as they drew near entered a small room and stood behind the door as they rushed by. He came out and ran swiftly and noiselessly in the other direction, and in a moment the steps were after him. He found the long corridor and raced along it at top speed. The stairs he knew were at the end, and with the steps close behind he descended them in blind haste. The steps gained on him, and he shrank to the side to let them pass, still continuing his headlong flight. Then suddenly he seemed to slip off the earth into space.

Lester awoke in the morning to find the sunshine streaming into the room, and White sitting up and regarding with some perplexity a badly-blistered finger.

'Where are the others?' inquired Lester.

'Gone, I suppose,' said White. 'We must have been asleep.'

Lester arose, and, stretching his stiffened limbs, dusted his clothes with his hands and went out into the corridor. White followed. At the noise of their approach a figure which had been lying asleep at the other end sat up and revealed the face of Barnes. 'Why, I've been asleep,' he said, in surprise. 'I don't remember coming here. How did I get here?'

'Nice place to come for a nap,' said Lester severely, as he pointed to the gap in the balusters. 'Look there! Another yard and where would you have been?'

He walked carelessly to the edge and looked over. In response to his startled cry the others drew near, and all three stood staring at the dead man below.

5

A CHANGE OF TREATMENT

'Yes, I've sailed under some 'cute skippers in my time,' said the night-watchman; 'them that go down in big ships see the wonders o' the deep, you know,' he added with a sudden chuckle, 'but the one I'm going to tell you about ought never to have been trusted out without 'is ma. A good many o' my skippers had fads, but this one was the worst I ever sailed under.

'It's some few years ago now; I'd shipped on his barque, the John Elliott, as slow-going an old tub as ever I was aboard of, when I wasn't in quite a fit an' proper state to know what I was doing, an' I hadn't been in her two days afore I found out his 'obby through overhearing a few remarks made by the second mate, who came up from dinner in a hurry to make 'em. "I don't mind saws an' knives hung round the cabin," he ses to the fust mate, "but when a chap has a 'uman 'and alongside 'is plate, studying it while folks is at their food, it's more than a Christian man can stand."

'"That's nothing," ses the fust mate, who had sailed with the barque afore. "He's half crazy on doctoring. We nearly had a mutiny aboard once owing to his wanting to hold a post-mortem on a man what fell from the mast-head. Wanted to see what the poor feller died of."

'"I call it unwholesome," ses the second mate very savage.

"He offered me a pill at breakfast the size of a small marble; quite put me off my feed, it did."

'Of course, the skipper's fad soon got known for'ard. But I didn't think much about it, till one day I seed old Dan'l Dennis sitting on a locker reading. Every now and then he'd shut the book, an' look up, closing 'is eyes, an' moving his lips like a hen drinking, an' then look down at the book again.

'"Why, Dan," I ses, "what's up? you ain't larning lessons at your time o' life?"

'"Yes, I am," ses Dan very soft. "You might hear me say it, it's this one about heart disease."

'He hands over the book, which was stuck full o' all kinds o' diseases, and winks at me 'ard.

'"Picked it up on a book-stall," he ses; then he shut 'is eyes an' said his piece wonderful. It made me quite queer to listen to 'im. "That's how I feel," ses he, when he'd finished. "Just strength enough to get to bed. Lend a hand, Bill, an' go an' fetch the doctor."

'Then I see his little game, but I wasn't going to run any risks, so I just mentioned, permiscous like, to the cook as old Dan seemed rather queer, an' went back an' tried to borrer the book, being always fond of reading. Old Dan pretended he was too ill to hear what I was saying, an' afore I could take it away from him, the skipper comes hurrying down with a bag in his 'and.

'"What's the matter, my man?" ses he, "what's the matter?"

'"I'm all right, sir," ses old Dan, "cept that I've been swoonding away a little."

'"Tell me exactly how you feel," ses the skipper, feeling his pulse.

'Then old Dan said his piece over to him, an' the skipper shook his head an' looked very solemn.

'"How long have you been like this?" he ses.

"'Four or five years, sir," ses Dan. "It ain't nothing serious, sir, is it?"

"'You lie quite still," ses the skipper, putting a little trumpet thing to his chest an' then listening. "Um! there's serious mischief here I'm afraid, the prognotice is very bad."

"'Prog what, sir?" ses Dan, staring.

"'Prognotice," ses the skipper, at least I think that's the word he said. "You keep perfectly still, an' I'll go an' mix you up a draught, and tell the cook to get some strong beef-tea on."

'Well, the skipper 'ad no sooner gone, than Cornish Harry, a great big lumbering chap o' six feet two, goes up to old Dan, an' he ses, "Gimme that book."

"'Go away," says Dan, "don't come worrying 'ere; you 'eard the skipper say how bad my prognotice was."

"'You lend me the book," ses Harry, ketching hold of him, "or else I'll bang you first, and split to the skipper arterwards. I believe I'm a bit consumptive. Anyway, I'm going to see."

'He dragged the book away from the old man, and began to study. There was so many complaints in it he was almost tempted to have something else instead of consumption, but he decided on that at last, an' he got a cough what worried the fo'c'sle all night long, an' the next day, when the skipper came down to see Dan, he could 'ardly 'ear hisself speak.

"'That's a nasty cough you've got, my man," ses he, looking at Harry.

"'Oh, it's nothing, sir," ses Harry, careless like. "I've 'ad it for months now off and on. I think it's perspiring so of a night does it."

"'What?" ses the skipper. "Do you perspire of a night?"

"'Dredful," ses Harry. "You could wring the clo'es out. I s'pose it's healthy for me, ain't it, sir?"

"'Undo your shirt," ses the skipper, going over to him, an' sticking the trumpet agin him. "Now take a deep breath.

Don't cough."

"'I can't help it, sir,' ses Harry, "it will come. Seems to tear me to pieces."

"'You get to bed at once,' says the skipper, taking away the trumpet, an' shaking his 'ed. "It's a fortunate thing for you, my lad, you're in skilled hands. With care, I believe I can pull you round. How does that medicine suit you, Dan?"

"'Beautiful, sir,' says Dan. "It's wonderful soothing, I slep' like a new-born babe arter it."

"'I'll send you some more,' ses the skipper. "You're not to get up mind, either of you."

"'All right, sir,' ses the two in very faint voices, an' the skipper went away arter telling us to be careful not to make a noise.

'We all thought it a fine joke at first, but the airs them two chaps give themselves was something sickening. Being in bed all day, they was naturally wakeful of a night, and they used to call across the fo'c'sle inquiring arter each other's healths, an' waking us other chaps up. An' they'd swop beef-tea an' jellies with each other, an' Dan 'ud try an' coax a little port wine out o' Harry, which he 'ad to make blood with, but Harry 'ud say he hadn't made enough that day, an' he'd drink to the better health of old Dan's prognotice, an' smack his lips until it drove us a'most crazy to 'ear him.

'Arter these chaps had been ill two days, the other fellers began to put their heads together, being maddened by the smell o' beef-tea an' the like, an' said they was going to be ill too, and both the invalids got into a fearful state of excitement.

"'You'll only spoil it for all of us,' ses Harry, "and you don't know what to have without the book."

"'It's all very well doing your work as well as our own,' ses one of the men. "It's our turn now. It's time you two got well."

"'WELL?' ses Harry, "well? Why you silly iggernerant

chaps, we shan't never get well, people with our complaints never do. You ought to know that."

"'Well, I shall split,' ses one of them. 'You do!' ses Harry, 'you do, an' I'll put a 'ed on you that all the port wine and jellies in the world wouldn't cure. 'Sides, don't you think the skipper knows what's the matter with us?'

'Afore the other chap could reply, the skipper hisself comes down, accompanied by the fust mate, with a look on his face which made Harry give the deepest and hollowest cough he'd ever done.

"'What they reely want,' ses the skipper, turning to the mate, 'is keerful nussing.'

"'I wish you'd let me nuss 'em,' ses the fust mate, 'only ten minutes—I'd put 'em both on their legs, an' running for their lives into the bargain, in ten minutes.'

"'Hold your tongue, sir,' ses the skipper; 'what you say is unfeeling, besides being an insult to me. Do you think I studied medicine all these years without knowing when a man's ill?'

'The fust mate growled something and went on deck, and the skipper started examining of 'em again. He said they was wonderfully patient lying in bed so long, an' he had 'em wrapped up in bedclo'es and carried on deck, so as the pure air could have a go at 'em. We had to do the carrying, an' there they sat, breathing the pure air, and looking at the fust mate out of the corners of their eyes. If they wanted anything from below one of us had to go an' fetch it, an' by the time they was taken down to bed again, we all resolved to be took ill too.

'Only two of 'em did it though, for Harry, who was a powerful, ugly-tempered chap, swore he'd do all sorts o' dreadful things to us if we didn't keep well and hearty, an' all 'cept these two did. One of 'em, Mike Rafferty, laid up with a swelling on his ribs, which I knew myself he 'ad 'ad for fifteen years, and the other chap had paralysis. I never saw a man so reely happy as the skipper was. He was up an down with his medicines and his instruments all day long, and used to make notes of the cases in a big pocket-book, and read 'em to the second mate at mealtimes.

'The fo'c'sle had been turned into hospital about a week, an' I was on deck doing some odd job or the other, when the cook comes up to me pulling a face as long as a fiddle.

'"Nother invalid," ses he; "fust mate's gone stark, staring mad!"

'"Mad?" ses I.

'"Yes," ses he. "He's got a big basin in the galley, an' he's laughing like a hyener an' mixing bilge-water an' ink, an' paraffin an' butter an' soap an' all sorts o' things up together. The smell's enough to kill a man; I've had to come away."

'Curious-like, I jest walked up to the galley an' puts my 'ed in, an' there was the mate as the cook said, smiling all over his face, and ladling some thick sticky stuff into a stone bottle.

'"How's the pore sufferers, sir?" ses he, stepping out of the galley jest as the skipper was going by.

'"They're very bad; but I hope for the best," ses the skipper, looking at him hard. "I'm glad to see you've turned a bit more feeling."

'"Yes, sir," ses the mate. "I didn't think so at fust, but I can see now them chaps is all very ill. You'll s'cuse me saying it, but I don't quite approve of your treatment."

'I thought the skipper would ha' bust.

'"My treatment?" ses he. "My treatment? What do you know about it?"

'"You're treating 'em wrong, sir," ses the mate. "I have here" (patting the jar) "a remedy which 'ud cure them all if you'd only let me try it."

'"Pooh!" ses the skipper. "One medicine cure all diseases! The old story. What is it? Where'd you get it from?" ses he.

A CHANGE OF TREATMENT 59

"'I brought the ingredients aboard with me,' ses the mate. "It's a wonderful medicine discovered by my grandmother, an' if I might only try it I'd thoroughly cure them pore chaps."

"'Rubbish!' ses the skipper.

"'Very well, sir,' ses the mate, shrugging his shoulders. "O' course, if you won't let me you won't. Still I tell you, if you'd let me try I'd cure 'em all in two days. That's a fair challenge."

'Well, they talked, and talked, and talked, until at last the skipper give way and went down below with the mate, and told the chaps they was to take the new medicine for two days, jest to prove the mate was wrong.

"'Let pore old Dan try it first, sir,' ses Harry, starting up, an' sniffing as the mate took the cork out; "he's been awful bad since you've been away."

"'Harry's worse than I am, sir,' ses Dan; "it's only his kind heart that makes him say that."

"'It don't matter which is fust,' ses the mate, filling a tablespoon with it, "there's plenty for all. Now, Harry."

"'Take it,' ses the skipper.

'Harry took it, an' the fuss he made you'd ha' thought he was swallering a football. It stuck all round his mouth, and he carried on so dredful that the other invalids was half sick afore it came to them.

'By the time the other three 'ad 'ad theirs it was as good as a pantermime, an' the mate corked the bottle up, and went an' sat down on a locker while they tried to rinse their mouths out with the luxuries which had been given 'em.

"'How do you feel?' ses the skipper.

"'I'm dying,' ses Dan.

"'So'm I,' ses Harry; "I b'leeve the mate's pisoned us."

'The skipper looks over at the mate very stern an' shakes his 'ed slowly.

"'It's all right,' ses the mate. "It's always like that the first dozen or so doses."

'"Dozen or so doses!" ses old Dan, in a far-away voice.

'"It has to be taken every twenty minutes," ses the mate, pulling out his pipe and lighting it; an' the four men groaned all together.

'"I can't allow it," ses the skipper, "I can't allow it. Men's lives mustn't be sacrificed for an experiment."

'"'T ain't a experiment," ses the mate very indignant, "it's an old family medicine."

'"Well, they shan't have any more," ses the skipper firmly.

'"Look here," ses the mate. "If I kill any one o' these men I'll give you twenty pound. Honour bright, I will."

'"Make it twenty-five," ses the skipper, considering.

'"Very good," ses the mate. "Twenty-five; I can't say no fairer than that, can I? It's about time for another dose now."

'He gave 'em another tablespoonful all round as the skipper left, an' the chaps what wasn't invalids nearly bust with joy. He wouldn't let 'em have anything to take the taste out, 'cos he said it didn't give the medicine a chance, an' he told us other chaps to remove the temptation, an' you bet we did.

'After the fifth dose, the invalids began to get desperate, an' when they heard they'd got to be woke up every twenty minutes through the night to take the stuff, they sort o' give up. Old Dan said he felt a gentle glow stealing over him and strengthening him, and Harry said that it felt like a healing balm to his lungs. All of 'em agreed it was a wonderful sort o' medicine, an' arter the sixth dose the man with paralysis dashed up on deck, and ran up the rigging like a cat. He sat there for hours spitting, an' swore he'd brain anybody who interrupted him, an' arter a little while Mike Rafferty went up and j'ined him, an' if the fust mate's ears didn't burn by reason of the things them two pore sufferers said about 'im, they ought to.

'They was all doing full work next day, an' though, o'course, the skipper saw how he'd been done, he didn't allude to it. Not in words, that is; but when a man tries to make four chaps do the work of eight, an' hits 'em when they don't, it's a easy job to see where the shoe pinches.'

6

THE CAPTAIN'S EXPLOIT

It was a wet, dreary night in that cheerless part of the great metropolis known as Wapping. The rain, which had been falling heavily for hours, still fell steadily on to the sloppy pavements and roads, and joining forces in the gutter, rushed impetuously to the nearest sewer. The two or three streets which had wedged themselves in between the docks and the river, and which, as a matter of fact, really comprise the beginning and end of Wapping, were deserted, except for a belated van crashing over the granite roads, or the chance form of a dock-labourer plodding doggedly along, with head bent in distaste for the rain, and hands sunk in trouser-pockets.

'Beastly night,' said Captain Bing, as he rolled out of the private bar of the "Sailor's Friend," and, ignoring the presence of the step, took a little hurried run across the pavement. 'Not fit for a dog to be out in.'

He kicked, as he spoke, at a shivering cur which was looking in at the crack of the bar-door, with a hazy view of calling its attention to the matter, and then, pulling up the collar of his rough pea-jacket, stepped boldly out into the rain. Three or four minutes' walk, or rather roll, brought him to a dark narrow passage, which ran between two houses to the water-side. By a slight tack to starboard at a critical moment he struck the channel safely, and followed it until it ended in a flight of old stone steps, half of which were under water.

'Where for?' inquired a man, starting up from a small penthouse formed of rough pieces of board.

'Schooner in the tier, Smiling Jane,' said the captain gruffly, as he stumbled clumsily into a boat and sat down in the stern. 'Why don't you have better seats in this 'ere boat?'

'They're there, if you'll look for them,' said the waterman; 'and you'll find 'em easier sitting than that bucket.'

'Why don't you put 'em where a man can see 'em?' inquired the captain, raising his voice a little.

The other opened his mouth to reply, but realising that it would lead to a long and utterly futile argument, contented himself with asking his fare to trim the boat better; and, pushing off from the steps, pulled strongly through the dark lumpy water. The tide was strong, so that they made but slow progress.

'When I was a young man,' said the fare with severity, 'I'd ha' pulled this boat across and back afore now.'

'When you was a young man,' said the man at the oars, who had a local reputation as a wit, 'there wasn't no boats; they was all Noah's arks then.'

'Stow your gab,' said the captain, after a pause of deep thought.

The other, whose besetting sin was certainly not loquacity, ejected a thin stream of tobacco-juice over the side, spat on his hands, and continued his laborious work until a crowd of dark shapes, surmounted by a network of rigging, loomed up before them.

'Now, which is your little barge?' he inquired, tugging strongly to maintain his position against the fast-flowing tide.

'Smiling Jane' said his fare.

'Ah,' said the waterman, 'Smiling Jane, is it? You sit there, cap'n, an' I'll row round all their sterns while you strike matches and look at the names. We'll have quite a nice little evening.'

'There she is,' cried the captain, who was too muddled to notice the sarcasm; 'there's the little beauty. Steady, my lad.'

He reached out his hand as he spoke, and as the boat jarred violently against a small schooner, seized a rope which hung over the side, and, swaying to and fro, fumbled in his pocket for the fare.

'Steady, old boy,' said the waterman affectionately. He had just received twopence-halfpenny and a shilling by mistake for threepence. 'Easy up the side. You ain't such a pretty figger as you was when your old woman made such a bad bargain.'

The captain paused in his climb, and poising himself on one foot, gingerly felt for his tormentor's head with the other. Not finding it, he flung his leg over the bulwark, and gained the deck of the vessel as the boat swung round with the tide and disappeared in the darkness.

'All turned in,' said the captain, gazing owlishly at the deserted deck. 'Well, there's a good hour an' a half afore we start; I'll turn in too.'

He walked slowly aft, and sliding back the companion-hatch, descended into a small evil-smelling cabin, and stood feeling in the darkness for the matches. They were not to be found, and, growling profanely, he felt his way to the state-room, and turned in all standing.

It was still dark when he awoke, and hanging over the edge of the bunk, cautiously felt for the floor with his feet, and having found it, stood thoughtfully scratching his head, which seemed to have swollen to abnormal proportions.

'Time they were getting under weigh,' he said at length, and groping his way to the foot of the steps, he opened the door of what looked like a small pantry, but which was really the mate's boudoir.

'Jem,' said the captain gruffly.

There was no reply, and jumping to the conclusion that he was above, the captain tumbled up the steps and gained the deck, which, as far as he could see, was in the same deserted condition as when he left it. Anxious to get some idea of the time, he staggered to the side and looked over. The tide was almost at the turn, and the steady clank, clank of neighbouring windlasses showed that other craft were just getting under weigh. A barge, its red light turning the water to blood, with a huge wall of dark sail, passed noiselessly by, the indistinct figure of a man leaning skilfully upon the tiller.

As these various signs of life and activity obtruded themselves upon the skipper of the Smiling Jane, his wrath rose higher and higher as he looked around the wet, deserted deck of his own little craft. Then he walked forward and thrust his head down the forecastle hatchway.

As he expected, there was a complete sleeping chorus below; the deep satisfied snoring of half-a-dozen seamen, who, regardless of the tide and their captain's feelings, were slumbering sweetly, in blissful ignorance of all that the Lancet might say upon the twin subjects of overcrowding and ventilation.

'Below there, you lazy thieves!' roared the captain; 'tumble up, tumble up!'

The snores stopped. 'Ay, ay!' said a sleepy voice. 'What's the matter, master?'

'Matter!' repeated the other, choking violently. 'Ain't you going to sail to-night?'

'To-night!' said another voice, in surprise. 'Why, I thought we wasn't going to sail till Wen'sday.'

Not trusting himself to reply, so careful was he of the morals of his men, the skipper went and leaned over the side and communed with the silent water. In an incredibly short space of time five or six dusky figures pattered up on to the deck, and a minute or two later the harsh clank of the windlass echoed far and wide.

The captain took the wheel. A fat and very sleepy seaman put up the side-lights, and the little schooner, detaching itself by the aid of boat-hooks and fenders from the neighbouring craft, moved slowly down with the tide. The men, in response to the captain's fervent orders, climbed aloft, and sail after sail was spread to the gentle breeze.

'Hi! you there,' cried the captain to one of the men who stood near him, coiling up some loose line.

'Sir?' said the man.

'Where is the mate?' inquired the captain.

'Man with red whiskers and pimply nose?' said the man interrogatively.

'That's him to a hair,' answered the other.

'Ain't seen him since he took me on at eleven,' said the man. 'How many new hands are there?'

'I b'leeve we're all fresh,' was the reply. 'I don't believe some of 'em have ever smelt salt water afore.'

'The mate's been at it again,' said the captain warmly, 'that's what he has. He's done it afore and got left behind. Them what can't stand drink, my man, shouldn't take it, remember that.'

'He said we wasn't going to sail till Wen'sday,' remarked the man, who found the captain's attitude rather trying.

'He'll get sacked, that's what he'll get,' said the captain warmly. 'I shall report him as soon as I get ashore.'

The subject exhausted, the seaman returned to his work, and the captain continued steering in moody silence.

Slowly, slowly darkness gave way to light. The different portions of the craft, instead of all being blurred into one, took upon themselves shape, and stood out wet and distinct in the cold grey of the breaking day. But the lighter it became, the harder the skipper stared and rubbed his eyes, and looked from the deck to the flat marshy shore, and from the shore back to the deck again.

'Here, come here,' he cried, beckoning to one of the crew.

'Yessir,' said the man, advancing.

'There's something in one of my eyes,' faltered the skipper. 'I can't see straight; everything seems mixed up. Now, speaking deliberate and without any hurry, which side o' the ship do you say the cook's galley's on?'

'Starboard,' said the man promptly, eyeing him with astonishment.

'Starboard,' repeated the other softly. 'He says starboard, and that's what it seems to me. My lad, yesterday morning it was on the port side.'

The seaman received this astounding communication with calmness, but, as a slight concession to appearances, said, 'Lor!'

'And the water-cask,' said the skipper; 'what colour is it?'

'Green,' said the man.

'Not white?' inquired the skipper, leaning heavily upon the wheel.

'Whitish-green,' said the man, who always believed in keeping in with his superior officers.

The captain swore at him.

By this time two or three of the crew who had over-heard part of the conversation had collected aft, and now stood in a small wondering knot before their strange captain.

'My lads,' said the latter, moistening his dry lips with his tongue, 'I name no names—I don't know 'em yet—and I cast no suspicions, but somebody has been painting up and altering this 'ere craft, and twisting things about until a man 'ud hardly know her. Now what's the little game?'

There was no answer, and the captain, who was seeing things clearer and clearer in the growing light, got paler and paler.

'I must be going crazy,' he muttered. 'Is this the Smiling Jane, or am I dreaming?'

'It ain't the Smiling Jane,' said one of the seamen; 'leastways,' he added cautiously, 'it wasn't when I came aboard.'

'Not the Smiling Jane!' roared the skipper; 'what is it, then?'

'Why, the Mary Ann,' chorused the astonished crew.

'My lads,' faltered the agonised captain after a long pause. 'My lads—' He stopped and swallowed something in his throat. 'I've been and brought away the wrong ship,' he continued with an effort; 'that's what I've done. I must have been bewitched.'

'Well, who's having the little game now?' inquired a voice.

'Somebody else'll be sacked as well as the mate,' said another.

'We must take her back,' said the captain, raising his voice to drown these mutterings. 'Stand by there!'

The bewildered crew went to their posts, the captain gave his orders in a voice which had never been so subdued and mellow since it broke at the age of fourteen, and the Mary Ann took in sail, and, dropping her anchor, waited patiently for the turning of the tide.

The church bells in Wapping and Rotherhithe were just striking the hour of mid-day, though they were heard by few above the noisy din of workers on wharves and ships, as a short stout captain, and a mate with red whiskers and a pimply nose, stood up in a waterman's boat in the centre of the river, and gazed at each other in blank astonishment.

'She's gone, clean gone!' murmured the bewildered captain.

'Clean as a whistle,' said the mate. 'The new hands must ha' run away with her.'

Then the bereaved captain raised his voice, and pronounced a pathetic and beautiful eulogy upon the departed vessel, somewhat marred by an appendix in which he consigned the new hands, their heirs, and descendants, to everlasting perdition.

'Ahoy!' said the waterman, who was getting tired of the business, addressing a grimy-looking seaman hanging meditatively over the side of a schooner. 'Where's the Mary Ann?'

'Went away at half-past one this morning,' was the reply.

"Cos here's the cap'n an' the mate,' said the waterman, indicating the forlorn couple with a bob of his head.

'My eyes!' said the man, 'I s'pose the cook's in charge then. We was to have gone too, but our old man hasn't turned up.'

Quickly the news spread amongst the craft in the tier, and many and various were the suggestions shouted to the bewildered couple from the different decks. At last, just as the captain had ordered the waterman to return to the shore, he was startled by a loud cry from the mate.

'Look there!' he shouted.

The captain looked. Fifty or sixty yards away, a small shamefaced-looking schooner, so it appeared to his excited imagination, was slowly approaching them. A minute later a shout went up from the other craft as she took in sail and bore slowly down upon them. Then a small boat put off to the buoy, and the Mary Ann was slowly warped into the place she had left ten hours before.

But while all this was going on, she was boarded by her captain and mate. They were met by Captain Bing, supported by his mate, who had hastily pushed off from the Smiling Jane to the assistance of his chief. In the two leading features before mentioned he was not unlike the mate of the Mary Ann, and much stress was laid upon this fact by the unfortunate Bing in his explanation. So much so, in fact, that both the mates got restless; the skipper, who was a plain man, and given to calling a spade a spade, using the word 'pimply' with what seemed to them unnecessary iteration.

It is possible that the interview might have lasted for hours had not Bing suddenly changed his tactics and begun to throw out dark hints about standing a dinner ashore, and settling it over a friendly glass. The face of the Mary Ann's captain began to clear, and, as Bing proceeded from generalities to details, a soft smile played over his expressive features. It was reflected in the faces of the mates, who by these means showed clearly that they understood the table was to be laid for four.

At this happy turn of affairs Bing himself smiled, and a little while later a ship's boat containing four boon companions put off from the Mary Ann and made for the shore. Of what afterwards ensued there is no distinct record, beyond what may be gleaned from the fact that the quartette turned up at midnight arm-in-arm, and affectionately refused to be separated—even to enter the ship's boat, which was waiting for them. The sailors were at first rather nonplussed, but by dint of much coaxing and argument broke up the party, and rowing them to their respective vessels, put them carefully to bed.

7

CONTRABAND OF WAR

A small but strong lamp was burning in the fo'c'sle of the schooner Greyhound, by the light of which a middle-aged seaman of sedate appearance sat crocheting an antimacassar. Two other men were snoring with deep content in their bunks, while a small, bright-eyed boy sat up in his, reading adventurous fiction.

'Here comes old Dan,' said the man with the anti macassar warningly, as a pair of sea boots appeared at the top of the companion-ladder; 'better not let him see you with that paper, Billee.'

The boy thrust it beneath his blankets, and, lying down, closed his eyes as the new-comer stepped on to the floor.

'All asleep?' inquired the latter.

The other man nodded, and Dan, without any further parley, crossed over to the sleepers and shook them roughly.

'Eh! wha's matter?' inquired the sleepers plaintively.

'Git up,' said Dan impressively, 'I want to speak to you. Something important.'

With sundry growls the men complied, and, thrusting their legs out of their bunks, rolled on to the locker, and sat crossly waiting for information.

'I want to do a pore chap a good turn,' said Dan, watching

them narrowly out of his little black eyes, 'an' I want you to help me; an' the boy too. It's never too young to do good to your fellow-creatures, Billy.'

'I know it ain't,' said Billy, taking this as permission to join the group; 'I helped a drunken man home once when I was only ten years old, an' when I was only—'

The speaker stopped, not because he had come to the end of his remarks, but because one of the seamen had passed his arm around his neck and was choking him.

'Go on,' said the man calmly; 'I've got him. Spit it out, Dan, and none of your sermonising.'

'Well, it's like this, Joe,' said the old man; 'here's a pore chap, a young sojer from the depot here, an' he's cut an' run. He's been in hiding in a cottage up the road two days, and he wants to git to London, and git honest work and employment, not shooting, an' stabbing, an' bayoneting—'

'Stow it,' said Joe impatiently.

'He daren't go to the railway station, and he dursen't go outside in his uniform,' continued Dan. 'My 'art bled for the pore young feller, an' I've promised to give 'im a little trip to London with us. The people he's staying with won't have him no longer. They've only got one bed, and directly he sees any sojers coming he goes an' gits into it, whether he's got his boots on or not.'

'Have you told the skipper?' inquired Joe sardonically.

'I won't deceive you, Joe, I 'ave not,' replied the old man. 'He'll have to stay down here of a daytime, an' only come on deck of a night when it's our watch. I told 'im what a lot of good 'arted chaps you was, and how—'

'How much is he going to give you?' inquired Joe impatiently.

'It's only fit and proper he should pay a little for the passage,' said Dan.

'How MUCH?' demanded Joe, banging the little triangular

table with his fist, and thereby causing the man with the antimacassar to drop a couple of stitches.

'Twenty-five shillings,' said old Dan reluctantly; 'an' I'll spend the odd five shillings on you chaps when we git to Limehouse.'

'I don't want your money,' said Joe; 'there's a empty bunk he can have; and mind, you take all the responsibility—I won't have nothing to do with it.'

'Thanks, Joe,' said the old man, with a sigh of relief; 'he's a nice young chap, you're sure to take to him. I'll go and give him the tip to come aboard at once.'

He ran up on deck again and whistled softly, and a figure, which had been hiding behind a pile of empties, came out, and, after looking cautiously around, dropped noiselessly on to the schooner's deck, and followed its protector below.

'Good evening, mates,' said the linesman, gazing curiously and anxiously round him as he deposited a bundle on the table, and laid his swagger cane beside it.

'What's your height?' inquired Joe abruptly. 'Seven foot?'

'No, only six foot four,' said the new arrival, modestly. 'I'm not proud of it. It's much easier for a small man to slip off than a big one.'

'It licks me,' said Joe thoughtfully, 'what they want 'em back for—I should think they'd be glad to git rid o' such'—he paused a moment while politeness struggled with feeling, and added, 'skunks.'

'P'raps I've a reason for being a skunk, p'raps I haven't,' retorted Private Smith, as his face fell.

'This'll be your bunk,' interposed Dan hastily; 'put your things in there, and when you are in yourself you'll be as comfortable as a oyster in its shell.'

The visitor complied, and, first extracting from the bundle some tins of meat and a bottle of whiskey, which he placed upon the table, nervously requested the honour of the present company to supper. With the exception of Joe, who churlishly climbed back into his bunk, the men complied, all agreeing that boys of Billy's age should be reared on strong teetotal principles.

Supper over, Private Smith and his protectors retired to their couches, where the former lay in much anxiety until two in the morning, when they got under way.

'It's all right, my lad,' said Dan, after the watch had been set, as he came and stood by the deserter's bunk; 'I've saved you—I've saved you for twenty-five shillings.'

'I wish it was more,' said Private Smith politely.

The old man sighed—and waited.

'I'm quite cleaned out, though,' continued the deserter, 'except fi'pence ha'penny. I shall have to risk going home in my uniform as it is.'

'Ah, you'll get there all right,' said Dan cheerfully; 'and when you get home no doubt you've got friends, and if it seems to you as you'd like to give a little more to them as assisted you in the hour of need, you won't be ungrateful, my lad, I know. You ain't the sort.'

With these words old Dan, patting him affectionately, retired, and the soldier lay trying to sleep in his narrow quarters until he was aroused by a grip on his arm.

'If you want a mouthful of fresh air you'd better come on deck now,' said the voice of Joe; 'it's my watch. You can get all the sleep you want in the daytime.'

Glad to escape from such stuffy quarters, Private Smith clambered out of his bunk and followed the other on deck. It was a fine clear night, and the schooner was going along under a light breeze; the seaman took the wheel, and, turning to his companion, abruptly inquired what he meant by deserting and worrying them with six foot four of underdone lobster.

'It's all through my girl,' said Private Smith meekly; 'first she jilted me, and made me join the army; now she's chucked the other fellow, and wrote to me to go back.'

'An' now I s'pose the other chap'll take your place in the army,' said Joe. 'Why, a gal like that could fill a regiment, if she liked. Pah! They'll nab you too, in that uniform, and you'll get six months, and have to finish your time as well.'

'It's more than likely,' said the soldier gloomily. 'I've got to tramp to Manchester in these clothes, as far as I can see.'

'What did you give old Dan all your money for?' inquired Joe.

'I was only thinking of getting away at first,' said Smith, 'and I had to take what was offered.'

'Well, I'll do what I can for you,' said the seaman. 'If you're in love, you ain't responsible for your actions. I remember the first time I got the chuck. I went into a public-house bar, and smashed all the glass and bottles I could get at. I felt as though I must do something. If you were only shorter, I'd lend you some clothes.'

'You're a brick,' said the soldier gratefully.

'I haven't got any money I could lend you either,' said Joe. 'I never do have any, somehow. But clothes you must have.'

He fell into deep thought, and cocked his eye aloft as though contemplating a cutting-out expedition on the sails, while the soldier, sitting on the side of the ship, waited hopefully for a miracle.

'You'd better get below again,' said Joe presently.

'There seems to be somebody moving below; and if the skipper sees you, you're done. He's a regular Tartar, and he's got a brother what's a sergeant-major in the army. He'd give you up d'rectly if he spotted you.'

'I'm off,' said Smith; and with long, cat-like strides he disappeared swiftly below.

For two days all went well, and Dan was beginning to congratulate himself upon his little venture, when his peace of mind was rudely disturbed. The crew were down below, having their tea, when Billy, who had been to the galley for hot water, came down, white and scared.

'Look here,' he said nervously, 'I've not had anything to do with this chap being aboard, have I?'

'What's the matter?' inquired Dan quickly.

'It's all found out,' said Billy.

'WHAT!' cried the crew simultaneously.

'Leastways, it will be,' said the youth, correcting himself. 'You'd better chuck him overboard while you've got time. I heard the cap'n tell the mate as he was coming down in the fo'c'sle to-morrow morning to look round. He's going to have it painted.'

'This,' said Dan, in the midst of a painful pause, 'this is what comes of helping a fellow-creature. What's to be done?'

'Tell the skipper the fo'c'sle don't want painting,' suggested Billy.

The agonised old seaman, carefully putting down his saucer of tea, cuffed his head spitefully.

'It's a smooth sea,' said he, looking at the perturbed countenance of Private Smith, 'an there's a lot of shipping about. If I was a deserter, sooner than be caught, I would slip overboard to-night with a lifebelt and take my chance.'

'I wouldn't,' said Mr Smith, with much decision.

'You wouldn't? Not if you was quite near another ship?' cooed Dan.

'Not if I was near fifty blooming ships, all trying to see which could pick me up first,' replied Mr Smith, with some heat.

'Then we shall have to leave you to your fate,' said Dan solemnly. 'If a man's unreasonable, his best friends can do nothing for him.'

'Chuck all his clothes overboard, anyway,' said Billy.

'That's a good idea o' the boy's. You leave his ears alone,' said Joe, stopping the ready hand of the exasperated Dan. 'He's got more sense than any of us. Can you think of anything else, Billy? What shall we do then?'

The eyes of all were turned upon their youthful deliverer, those of Mr Smith being painfully prominent. It was a proud moment for Billy, and he sat silent for some time, with a look of ineffable wisdom and thought upon his face. At length he spoke.

'Let somebody else have a turn,' he said generously.

The voice of the antimacassar worker broke the silence.

'Paint him all over with stripes of different-coloured paint, and let him pretend he's mad, and didn't know how he got here,' he said, with an uncontrollable ring of pride at the idea, which was very coldly received, Private Smith being noticeably hard on it.

'I know,' said Billy shrilly, clapping his hands. 'I've got it, I've got it. After he's chucked his clothes overboard to-night, let him go overboard too, with a line.'

'And tow him the rest o' the way, and chuck biscuits to him, I suppose,' snarled Dan.

'No,' said the youthful genius scornfully; 'pretend he's been upset from a boat, and has been swimming about, and we heard him cry out for help and rescued him.'

'It's about the best way out of it,' said Joe, after some deliberation; 'it's warm weather, and you won't take no harm, mate. Do it in my watch, and I'll pull you out directly.'

'Wouldn't it do if you just chucked a bucket of water over me and SAID you'd pulled me out,' suggested the victim. 'The other thing seems a downright LIE.'

'No,' said Billy authoritatively, 'you've got to look half-drowned, and swallow a lot of water, and your eyes be all bloodshot.'

Everybody being eager for the adventure, except Private Smith, the arrangements were at once concluded, and the approach of night impatiently awaited. It was just before midnight when Smith, who had forgotten for the time his troubles in sleep, was shaken into wakefulness.

'Cold water, sir?' said Billy gleefully.

In no mood for frivolity, Private Smith rose and followed the youth on deck. The air struck him as chill as he stood there; but, for all that, it was with a sense of relief that he saw Her Majesty's uniform go over the side and sink into the dark water.

'He don't look much with his padding off, does he?' said Billy, who had been eyeing him critically.

'You go below,' said Dan sharply.

'Garn,' said Billy indignantly; 'I want to see the fun as well as you do. I thought of it.'

'Fun?' said the old man severely. 'Fun? To see a feller creature suffering, and perhaps drowned—'

'I don't think I had better go,' said the victim; 'it seems rather underhand.'

'Yes, you will,' said Joe. 'Wind this line round an' round your arm, and just swim about gently till I pull you in.'

Sorely against his inclination Private Smith took hold of the line, and, hanging over the side of the schooner, felt the temperature with his foot, and, slowly and tenderly, with many little gasps, committed his body to the deep. Joe paid out the line and waited, letting out more line, when the man in the water, who was getting anxious, started to come in hand over hand.

'That'll do,' said Dan at length.

'I think it will,' said Joe, and, putting his hand to his mouth, gave a mighty shout. It was answered almost directly by startled roars from the cabin, and the skipper and mate came rushing hastily upon deck, to see the crew, in their sleeping gear, forming an excited group round Joe, and peering eagerly over the side.

'What's the matter?' demanded the skipper.

'Somebody in the water, sir,' said Joe, relinquishing the wheel to one of the other seamen, and hauling in the line. 'I heard a cry from the water and threw a line, and, by gum, I've hooked it!'

He hauled in, lustily aided by the skipper, until the long white body of Private Smith, blanched with the cold, came bumping against the schooner's side.

'It's a mermaid,' said the mate, who was inclined to be superstitious, as he peered doubtfully down at it. 'Let it go, Joe.'

'Haul it in, boys,' said the skipper impatiently; and two of the men clambered over the side and, stooping down, raised it from the water.

In the midst of a puddle, which he brought with him, Private Smith was laid on the deck, and, waving his arms about, fought wildly for his breath.

'Fetch one of them empties,' said the skipper quickly, as he pointed to some barrels ranged along the side.

The men rolled one over, and then aided the skipper in placing the long fair form of their visitor across it, and to trundle it lustily up and down the deck, his legs forming convenient handles for the energetic operators.

'He's coming round,' said the mate, checking them; 'he's speaking. How do you feel, my poor fellow?'

He put his ear down, but the action was unnecessary. Private Smith felt bad, and, in the plainest English he could think of at the moment, said so distinctly.

'He's swearing,' said the mate. 'He ought to be ashamed

of himself.'

'Yes,' said the skipper austerely; 'and him so near death too. How did you get in the water?'

'Went for a—swim,' panted Smith surlily.

'SWIM?' echoed the skipper. 'Why, we're ten miles from land!'

'His mind's wandering, pore feller,' interrupted Joe hurriedly. 'What boat did you fall out of, matey?'

'A row-boat,' said Smith, trying to roll out of reach of the skipper, who was down on his knees flaying him alive with a roller-towel. 'I had to undress in the water to keep afloat. I've lost all my clothes.'

'Pore feller,' said Dan.

'A gold watch and chain, my purse, and three of the nicest fellers that ever breathed,' continued Smith, who was now entering into the spirit of the thing.

'Poor chaps,' said the skipper solemnly. 'Any of 'em leave any family?'

'Four,' said Smith sadly.

'Children?' queried the mate.

'Families,' said Smith.

'Look here,' said the mate, but the watchful Joe interrupted him.

'His mind's wandering,' said he hastily. 'He can't count, pore chap. We'd better git him to bed.'

'Ah, do,' said the skipper, and, assisted by his friends, the rescued man was half led, half carried below and put between the blankets, where he lay luxuriously sipping a glass of brandy and water, sent from the cabin.

'How'd I do it?' he inquired, with a satisfied air.

'There was no need to tell all them lies about it,' said Dan sharply; 'instead of one little lie you told half-a-dozen. I don't want nothing more to do with you. You start afresh now, like a new-born babe.'

'All right,' said Smith shortly; and, being very much fatigued with his exertions, and much refreshed by the brandy, fell into a deep and peaceful sleep.

The morning was well advanced when he awoke, and the fo'c'sle empty except for the faithful Joe, who was standing by his side, with a heap of clothing under his arm.

'Try these on,' said he, as Smith stared at him half awake; 'they'll be better than nothing, at any rate.'

The soldier leaped from his bunk and gratefully proceeded to dress himself, Joe eyeing him critically as the trousers climbed up his long legs, and the sleeves of the jacket did their best to conceal his elbows.

'What do I look like?' he inquired anxiously, as he finished.

'Six foot an' a half o' misery,' piped the shrill voice of Billy promptly, as he thrust his head in at the fo'c'sle. 'You can't go to church in those clothes.'

'Well, they'll do for the ship, but you can't go ashore in 'em,' said Joe, as he edged towards the ladder, and suddenly sprang up a step or two to let fly at the boy, 'The old man wants to see you; be careful what you say to him.'

With a very unsuccessful attempt to appear unconscious of the figure he cut, Smith went up on deck for the interview.

'We can't do anything until we get to London,' said the skipper, as he made copious notes of Smith's adventures. 'As soon as we get there, I'll lend you the money to telegraph to your friends to tell 'em you're safe and to send you some clothes, and of course you'll have free board and lodging till it comes, and I'll write out an account of it for the newspapers.'

'You're very good,' said Smith blankly.

'And I don't know what you are,' said the skipper, interrogatively; 'but you ought to go in for swimming as a profession—six hours' swimming about like that is wonderful.'

'You don't know what you can do till you have to,' said Smith modestly, as he backed slowly away; 'but I never want to see the water again as long as I live.'

The two remaining days of their passage passed all too quickly for the men, who were casting about for some way out of the difficulty which they foresaw would arise when they reached London.

'If you'd only got decent clothes,' said Joe, as they passed Gravesend, 'you could go off and send a telegram, and not come back; but you couldn't go five yards in them things without having a crowd after you.'

'I shall have to be taken I s'pose,' said Smith moodily.

'An' poor old Dan'll get six months hard for helping you off,' said Joe sympathetically, as a bright idea occurred to him.

'Rubbish!' said Dan uneasily. 'He can stick to his tale of being upset; anyway, the skipper saw him pulled out of the water. He's too honest a chap to get an old man into trouble for trying to help him.'

'He must have a new rig out, Dan,' said Joe softly. 'You an' me'll go an' buy 'em. I'll do the choosing, and you'll do the paying. Why, it'll be a reg'lar treat for you to lay out a little money, Dan. We'll have quite an evening's shopping, everything of the best.'

The infuriated Dan gasped for breath, and looked helplessly at the grinning crew.

'I'll see him—overboard first,' he said furiously.

'Please yourself,' said Joe shortly, 'If he's caught you'll get six months. As it is, you've got a chance of doing a nice, kind little Christian act, becos, o' course, that twenty-five bob you got out of him won't anything like pay for his toggery.'

Almost beside himself with indignation, the old man moved off, and said not another word until they were made fast to the wharf at Limehouse. He did not even break silence when Joe, taking him affectionately by the arm, led him aft to the skipper.

'Me an' Dan, sir,' said Joe very respectfully, 'would like to go ashore for a little shopping. Dan has very kindly offered to lend that pore chap the money for some clothes, and he wants me to go with him to help carry them.'

'Ay, ay,' said the skipper, with a benevolent smile at the aged philanthropist. 'You'd better go at once, afore the shops shut.'

'We'll run, sir,' said Joe, and taking Dan by the arm, dragged him into the street at a trot.

Nearly a couple of hours passed before they returned, and no child watched with greater eagerness the opening of a birthday present than Smith watched the undoing of the numerous parcels with which they were laden.

'He's a reg'lar fairy godmother, ain't he?' said Joe, as Smith joyously dressed himself in a very presentable tweed suit, serviceable boots, and a bowler hat. 'We had a dreadful job to get a suit big enough, an' the only one we could get was rather more money than we wanted to give, wasn't it, Dan?'

The fairy godmother strove manfully with his feelings.

'You'll do now,' said Joe. 'I ain't got much, but what I have you're welcome to.' He put his hand into his pocket and pulled out some loose coin. 'What have you got, mates?'

With decent good-will the other men turned out their pockets, and, adding to the store, heartily pressed it upon the reluctant Smith, who, after shaking hands gratefully, followed Joe on deck.

'You've got enough to pay your fare,' said the latter; 'an' I've told the skipper you are going ashore to send off telegrams. If you send the money back to Dan, I'll never forgive you.'

'I won't, then,' said Smith firmly; 'but I'll send theirs back to the other chaps. Good-bye.'

Joe shook him by the hand again, and bade him go while

the coast was clear, advice which Smith hastened to follow, though he turned and looked back to wave his hand to the crew, who had come up on deck silently to see him off; all but the philanthropist, who was down below with a stump of lead-pencil and a piece of paper doing sums.

8

A BLACK AFFAIR

'I didn't want to bring it,' said Captain Gubson, regarding somewhat unfavourably a grey parrot whose cage was hanging against the mainmast, 'but my old uncle was so set on it I had to. He said a sea-voyage would set its 'elth up.'

'It seems to be all right at present,' said the mate, who was tenderly sucking his forefinger; 'best of spirits, I should say.'

'It's playful,' assented the skipper. 'The old man thinks a rare lot of it. I think I shall have a little bit in that quarter, so keep your eye on the beggar.'

'Scratch Poll!' said the parrot, giving its bill a preliminary strop on its perch. 'Scratch poor Polly!'

It bent its head against the bars, and waited patiently to play off what it had always regarded as the most consummate practical joke in existence. The first doubt it had ever had about it occurred when the mate came forward and obligingly scratched it with the stem of his pipe. It was a wholly unforeseen development, and the parrot, ruffling its feathers, edged along its perch and brooded darkly at the other end of it.

Opinion before the mast was also against the new arrival, the general view being that the wild jealousy which raged in the bosom of the ship's cat would sooner or later lead to mischief.

'Old Satan don't like it,' said the cook, shaking his head.

'The blessed bird hadn't been aboard ten minutes before Satan was prowling around. The blooming image waited till he was about a foot off the cage, and then he did the perlite and asked him whether he'd like a glass o' beer. I never see a cat so took aback in all my life. Never.'

'There'll be trouble between 'em,' said old Sam, who was the cat's special protector, 'mark my words.'

'I'd put my money on the parrot,' said one of the men confidently. 'It's 'ad a crool bit out of the mate's finger. Where 'ud the cat be agin that beak?'

'Well, you'd lose your money,' said Sam. 'If you want to do the cat a kindness, every time you see him near that cage cuff his 'ed.'

The crew being much attached to the cat, which had been presented to them when a kitten by the mate's wife, acted upon the advice with so much zest that for the next two days the indignant animal was like to have been killed with kindness. On the third day, however, the parrot's cage being on the cabin table, the cat stole furtively down, and, at the pressing request of the occupant itself, scratched its head for it.

The skipper was the first to discover the mischief, and he came on deck and published the news in a voice which struck a chill to all hearts.

'Where's that black devil got to?' he yelled.

'Anything wrong, sir?' asked Sam anxiously.

'Come and look here,' said the skipper. He led the way to the cabin, where the mate and one of the crew were already standing, shaking their heads over the parrot.

'What do you make of that?' demanded the skipper fiercely. 'Too much dry food, sir,' said Sam, after due deliberation. 'Too much what?' bellowed the skipper. 'Too much dry food,' repeated Sam firmly. 'A parrot—a grey parrot—wants plenty o' sop. If it don't get it, it moults.' 'It's had too much CAT' said the skipper fiercely, 'and you know it, and overboard it goes.'

'I don't believe it was the cat, sir,' interposed the other man; 'it's too soft-hearted to do a thing like that.'

'You can shut your jaw,' said the skipper, reddening. 'Who asked you to come down here at all?'

'Nobody saw the cat do it,' urged the mate.

The skipper said nothing, but, stooping down, picked up a tail feather from the floor, and laid it on the table. He then went on deck, followed by the others, and began calling, in seductive tones, for the cat. No reply forth coming from the sagacious animal, which had gone into hiding, he turned to Sam, and bade him call it.

'No, sir, I won't 'ave no 'and in it,' said the old man. 'Putting aside my liking for the animal, I'm not going to 'ave anything to do with the killing of a black cat.'

'Rubbish!' said the skipper.

'Very good, sir,' said Sam, shrugging his shoulders, 'you know best, o' course. You're eddicated and I'm not, an' p'raps you can afford to make a laugh o' such things. I knew one man who killed a black cat an' he went mad. There's something very pecooliar about that cat o' ours.'

'It knows more than we do,' said one of the crew, shaking his head. 'That time you—I mean we—ran the smack down, that cat was expecting of it 'ours before. It was like a wild thing.'

'Look at the weather we've 'ad—look at the trips we've made since he's been aboard,' said the old man. 'Tell me it's chance if you like, but I KNOW better.'

The skipper hesitated. He was a superstitious man even for a sailor, and his weakness was so well known that he had become a sympathetic receptacle for every ghost story which, by reason of its crudeness or lack of corroboration, had been rejected by other experts. He was a perfect reference library for omens, and his interpretations of dreams had gained for him a widespread reputation.

'That's all nonsense,' he said, pausing uneasily; 'still, I only want to be just. There's nothing vindictive about me, and I'll have no hand in it myself. Joe, just tie a lump of coal to that cat and heave it overboard.'

'Not me,' said the cook, following Sam's lead, and working up a shudder. 'Not for fifty pun in gold. I don't want to be haunted.'

'The parrot's a little better now, sir,' said one of the men, taking advantage of his hesitation, 'he's opened one eye.'

'Well, I only want to be just,' repeated the skipper. 'I won't do anything in a hurry, but, mark my words, if the parrot dies that cat goes overboard.'

Contrary to expectations, the bird was still alive when London was reached, though the cook, who from his connection with the cabin had suddenly reached a position of unusual importance, reported great loss of strength and irritability of temper. It was still alive, but failing fast on the day they were to put to sea again; and the fo'c'sle, in preparation for the worst, stowed their pet away in the paint-locker, and discussed the situation.

Their council was interrupted by the mysterious behaviour of the cook, who, having gone out to lay in a stock of bread, suddenly broke in upon them more in the manner of a member of a secret society than a humble but useful unit of a ship's company.

'Where's the cap'n?' he asked in a hoarse whisper, as he took a seat on the locker with the sack of bread between his knees.

'In the cabin,' said Sam, regarding his antics with some disfavour. 'What's wrong, cookie?'

'What d' yer think I've got in here?' asked the cook, patting

A BLACK AFFAIR

the bag.

The obvious reply to this question was, of course, bread; but as it was known that the cook had departed specially to buy some, and that he could hardly ask a question involving such a simple answer, nobody gave it.

'It come to me all of a sudden,' said the cook, in a thrilling whisper. 'I'd just bought the bread and left the shop, when I see a big black cat, the very image of ours, sitting on a doorstep. I just stooped down to stroke its 'ed, when it come to me.'

'They will sometimes,' said one of the seamen.

'I don't mean that,' said the cook, with the contempt of genius. 'I mean the idea did. Ses I to myself, "You might be old Satan's brother by the look of you; an' if the cap'n wants to kill a cat, let it be you," I ses. And with that, before it could say Jack Robinson, I picked it up by the scruff o' the neck and shoved it in the bag.'

'What, all in along of our bread?' said the previous interrupter, in a pained voice.

'Some of yer are 'ard ter please,' said the cook, deeply offended.

'Don't mind him, cook,' said the admiring Sam. 'You're a masterpiece, that's what you are.'

'Of course, if any of you've got a better plan'—said the cook generously.

'Don't talk rubbish, cook,' said Sam; 'fetch the two cats out and put 'em together.'

'Don't mix 'em,' said the cook warningly; 'for you'll never know which is which agin if you do.'

He cautiously opened the top of the sack and produced his captive, and Satan, having been relieved from his prison, the two animals were carefully compared.

'They're as like as two lumps o' coal,' said Sam slowly. 'Lord, what a joke on the old man. I must tell the mate o' this; he'll enjoy it.'

'It'll be all right if the parrot don't die,' said the dainty pessimist, still harping on his pet theme. 'All that bread spoilt, and two cats aboard.'

'Don't mind what he ses,' said Sam; 'you're a brick, that's what you are. I'll just make a few holes in the lid o' the boy's chest, and pop old Satan in. You don't mind, do you, Billy?'

'Of course he don't,' said the other men indignantly.

Matters being thus agreeably arranged, Sam got a gimlet, and prepared the chest for the reception of its tenant, who, convinced that he was being put out of the way to make room for a rival, made a frantic fight for freedom.

'Now get something 'eavy and put on the top of it,' said Sam, having convinced himself that the lock was broken; 'and, Billy, put the noo cat in the paint-locker till we start; it's homesick.'

The boy obeyed, and the understudy was kept in durance vile until they were off Limehouse, when he came on deck and nearly ended his career there and then by attempting to jump over the bulwark into the next garden. For some time he paced the deck in a perturbed fashion, and then, leaping on the stern, mewed plaintively as his native city receded farther and farther from his view.

'What's the matter with old Satan?' said the mate, who had been let into the secret. 'He seems to have something on his mind.'

'He'll have something round his neck presently,' said the skipper grimly.

The prophecy was fulfilled some three hours later, when he came up on deck ruefully regarding the remains of a bird whose vocabulary had once been the pride of its native town. He threw it overboard without a word, and then, seizing the innocent cat, who had followed him under the impression that it was about to lunch, produced half a brick attached to a string, and tied it round his neck. The crew, who were enjoying the joke immensely, raised a howl of protest.

'The Skylark'll never have another like it, sir,' said Sam solemnly. 'That cat was the luck of the ship.'

'I don't want any of your old woman's yarns,' said the skipper brutally. 'If you want the cat, go and fetch it.'

He stepped aft as he spoke, and sent the gentle stranger hurtling through the air. There was a 'plomp' as it reached the water, a bubble or two came to the surface, and all was over.

'That's the last o' that,' he said, turning away.

The old man shook his head. 'You can't kill a black cat for nothing,' said he, 'mark my words!'

The skipper, who was in a temper at the time, thought little of them, but they recurred to him vividly the next day. The wind had freshened during the night, and rain was falling heavily. On deck the crew stood about in oilskins, while below, the boy, in his new capacity of gaoler, was ministering to the wants of an ungrateful prisoner, when the cook, happening to glance that way, was horrified to see the animal emerge from the fo'c'sle. It eluded easily the frantic clutch of the boy as he sprang up the ladder after it, and walked leisurely along the deck in the direction of the cabin. Just as the crew had given it up for lost it encountered Sam, and the next moment, despite its cries, was caught up and huddled away beneath his stiff clammy oilskins. At the noise the skipper, who was talking to the mate, turned as though he had been shot, and gazed wildly round him.

'Dick,' said he, 'can you hear a cat?'

'Cat!' said the mate, in accents of great astonishment.

'I thought I heard it,' said the puzzled skipper.

'Fancy, sir,' said Dick firmly, as a mewing, appalling in its wrath, came from beneath Sam's coat.

'Did you hear it, Sam?' called the skipper, as the old man was moving off.

'Hear what, sir?' inquired Sam respectfully, without turning round.

'Nothing,' said the skipper, collecting himself. 'Nothing. All right.'

The old man, hardly able to believe in his good fortune, made his way forward, and, seizing a favourable opportunity, handed his ungrateful burden back to the boy.

'Fancy you heard a cat just now?' inquired the mate casually.

'Well, between you an' me, Dick,' said the skipper, in a mysterious voice, 'I did, and it wasn't fancy neither. I heard that cat as plain as if it was alive.'

'Well, I've heard of such things,' said the other, 'but I don't believe 'em. What a lark if the old cat comes back climbing up over the side out of the sea to-night, with the brick hanging round its neck.'

The skipper stared at him for some time without speaking. 'If that's your idea of a lark,' he said at length, in a voice which betrayed traces of some emotion, 'it ain't mine.'

'Well, if you hear it again,' said the mate cordially, 'you might let me know. I'm rather interested in such things.'

The skipper, hearing no more of it that day, tried hard to persuade himself that he was the victim of imagination, but, in spite of this, he was pleased at night, as he stood at the wheel, to reflect on the sense of companionship afforded by the lookout in the bows. On his part the look-out was quite charmed with the unwonted affability of the skipper, as he yelled out to him two or three times on matters only faintly connected with the progress of the schooner.

The night, which had been dirty, cleared somewhat, and the bright crescent of the moon appeared above a heavy bank of clouds, as the cat, which had by dint of using its back as a lever at length got free from that cursed chest, licked its shapely limbs, and came up on deck. After its stifling prison, the air was simply delicious.

'Bob!' yelled the skipper suddenly.

'Ay, ay, sir!' said the look-out, in a startled voice.

'Did you mew?' inquired the skipper.

'Did I WOT, sir?' cried the astonished Bob.

'Mew,' said the skipper sharply, 'like a cat?'

'No, sir,' said the offended seaman. 'What 'ud I want to do that for?'

'I don't know what you want to for,' said the skipper, looking round him uneasily. 'There's some more rain coming, Bob.'

'Ay, ay, sir,' said Bob.

'Lot o' rain we've had this summer,' said the skipper, in a meditative bawl.

'Ay, ay, sir,' said Bob. 'Sailing-ship on the port bow, sir.'

The conversation dropped, the skipper, anxious to divert his thoughts, watching the dark mass of sail as it came plunging out of the darkness into the moonlight until it was abreast of his own craft. His eyes followed it as it passed his quarter, so that he saw not the stealthy approach of the cat which came from behind the companion, and sat down close by him. For over thirty hours the animal had been subjected to the grossest indignities at the hands of every man on board the ship except one. That one was the skipper, and there is no doubt but that its subsequent behaviour was a direct recognition of that fact. It rose to its feet, and crossing over to the unconscious skipper, rubbed its head affectionately and vigorously against his leg.

From simple causes great events do spring. The skipper sprang four yards, and let off a screech which was the subject of much comment on the barque which had just passed. When Bob, who came shuffling up at the double, reached him he was leaning against the side, incapable of speech, and shaking all over.

'Anything wrong, sir?' inquired the seaman anxiously, as he ran to the wheel.

The skipper pulled himself together a bit, and got closer to his companion.

'Believe me or not, Bob,' he said at length, in trembling accents, 'just as you please, but the ghost of that—cat, I mean the ghost of that poor affectionate animal which I drowned, and which I wish I hadn't, came and rubbed itself up against my leg.'

'Which leg?' inquired Bob, who was ever careful about details.

'What the blazes does it matter which leg?' demanded the skipper, whose nerves were in a terrible state. 'Ah, look—look there!'

The seaman followed his outstretched finger, and his heart failed him as he saw the cat, with its back arched, gingerly picking its way along the side of the vessel.

'I can't see nothing,' he said doggedly.

'I don't suppose you can, Bob,' said the skipper in a melancholy voice, as the cat vanished in the bows; 'it's evidently only meant for me to see. What it means I don't know. I'm going down to turn in. I ain't fit for duty. You don't mind being left alone till the mate comes up, do you?'

'I ain't afraid,' said Bob.

His superior officer disappeared below, and, shaking the sleepy mate, who protested strongly against the proceedings, narrated in trembling tones his horrible experiences.

'If I were you '—said the mate.

'Yes?' said the skipper, waiting a bit. Then he shook him again, roughly.

'What were you going to say?' he inquired.

'Say?' said the mate, rubbing his eyes. 'Nothing.'

'About the cat?' suggested the skipper.

'Cat?' said the mate, nestling lovingly down in the blankets again. 'Wha' ca'—goo' ni''—

Then the skipper drew the blankets from the mate's sleepy clutches, and, rolling him backwards and forwards in the bunk, patiently explained to him that he was very unwell, that he was going to have a drop of whiskey neat, and turn in, and that he, the mate, was to take the watch. From this moment the joke lost much of its savour for the mate.

'You can have a nip too, Dick,' said the skipper, proffering him the whiskey, as the other sullenly dressed himself.

'It's all rot,' said the mate, tossing the spirits down his throat, 'and it's no use either; you can't run away from a ghost; it's just as likely to be in your bed as anywhere else. Good-night.'

He left the skipper pondering over his last words, and dubiously eyeing the piece of furniture in question. Nor did he retire until he had subjected it to an analysis of the most searching description, and then, leaving the lamp burning, he sprang hastily in, and forgot his troubles in sleep.

It was day when he awoke, and went on deck to find a heavy sea running, and just sufficient sail set to keep the schooner's head before the wind as she bobbed about on the waters. An exclamation from the skipper, as a wave broke against the side and flung a cloud of spray over him, brought the mate's head round.

'Why, you ain't going to get up?' he said, in tones of insincere surprise.

'Why not?' inquired the other gruffly.

'You go and lay down agin,' said the mate, 'and have a cup o' nice hot tea an' some toast.'

'Clear out,' said the skipper, making a dash for the wheel, and reaching it as the wet deck suddenly changed its angle. 'I know you didn't like being woke up, Dick; but I got the horrors last night. Go below and turn in.'

'All right,' said the mollified mate.

'You didn't see anything?' inquired the skipper, as he took the wheel from him.

'Nothing at all,' said the other.

The skipper shook his head thoughtfully, then shook it again vigorously, as another shower-bath put its head over the side and saluted him.

'I wish I hadn't drowned that cat, Dick,' he said.

'You won't see it again,' said Dick, with the confidence of a man who had taken every possible precaution to render the prophecy a safe one.

He went below, leaving the skipper at the wheel idly watching the cook as he performed marvellous feats of jugglery, between the galley and the fo'c'sle, with the men's breakfast.

A little while later, leaving the wheel to Sam, he went below himself and had his own, talking freely, to the discomfort of the conscious-stricken cook, about his weird experiences of the night before.

'You won't see it no more, sir, I don't expect,' he said faintly; 'I b'leeve it come and rubbed itself up agin your leg to show it forgave you.'

'Well, I hope it knows it's understood,' said the other. 'I don't want it to take any more trouble.'

He finished the breakfast in silence, and then went on deck again. It was still blowing hard, and he went over to superintend the men who were attempting to lash together some empties which were rolling about in all directions amidships. A violent roll set them free again, and at the same time separated two chests in the fo'c'sle, which were standing one on top of the other. This enabled Satan, who was crouching in the lower one, half crazed with terror, to come flying madly up on deck and give his feelings full vent. Three times in full view of the horrified skipper he circled the deck at racing speed, and had just started on the fourth when a heavy packing-case, which had been temporarily set on end and abandoned by the men at his sudden appearance, fell over and caught him by the tail. Sam rushed to the rescue.

'Stop!' yelled the skipper.

'Won't I put it up, sir?' inquired Sam.

'Do you see what's beneath it?' said the skipper, in a husky voice.

'Beneath it, sir?' said Sam, whose ideas were in a whirl.

'The cat, can't you see the cat?' said the skipper, whose eyes had been riveted on the animal since its first appearance on deck.

Sam hesitated a moment, and then shook his head.

'The case has fallen on the cat,' said the skipper. 'I can see it distinctly.'

He might have said heard it, too, for Satan was making frenzied appeals to his sympathetic friends for assistance.

'Let me put the case back, sir,' said one of the men, 'then p'raps the vision'll disappear.'

'No, stop where you are,' said the skipper. 'I can stand it better by daylight. It's the most wonderful and extraordinary thing I've ever seen. Do you mean to say you can't see anything, Sam?'

'I can see a case, sir,' said Sam, speaking slowly and carefully, 'with a bit of rusty iron band sticking out from it. That's what you're mistaking for the cat, p'raps, sir.'

'Can't you see anything, cook?' demanded the skipper.

'It may be fancy, sir,' faltered the cook, lowering his eyes, 'but it does seem to me as though I can see a little misty sort o' thing there. Ah, now it's gone.'

'No, it ain't,' said the skipper. 'The ghost of Satan's sitting there. The case seems to have fallen on its tail. It appears to be howling something dreadful.'

The men made a desperate effort to display the astonishment suitable to such a marvel, whilst Satan, who was trying all he knew to get his tail out, cursed freely. How long the superstitious captain of the Skylark would have let him remain there will never be known, for just then the mate came on deck and caught sight of it before he was quite aware of the part he was expected to play.

'Why the devil don't you lift the thing off the poor brute,' he yelled, hurrying up towards the case.

'What, can YOU see it, Dick?' said the skipper impressively, laying his hand on his arm.

'SEE it?' retorted the mate. 'D'ye think I'm blind. Listen to the poor brute. I should—Oh!'

He became conscious of the concentrated significant gaze of the crew. Five pairs of eyes speaking as one, all saying 'idiot' plainly, the boy's eyes conveying an expression too great to be translated.

Turning, the skipper saw the bye-play, and a light slowly dawned upon him. But he wanted more, and he wheeled suddenly to the cook for the required illumination.

The cook said it was a lark. Then he corrected himself and said it wasn't a lark, then he corrected himself again and became incoherent. Meantime the skipper eyed him stonily, while the mate released the cat and good-naturedly helped to straighten its tail.

It took fully five minutes of unwilling explanation before the skipper could grasp the situation. He did not appear to fairly understand it until he was shown the chest with the ventilated lid; then his countenance cleared, and, taking the unhappy Billy by the collar, he called sternly for a piece of rope.

By this statesmanlike handling of the subject a question

of much delicacy and difficulty was solved, discipline was preserved, and a practical illustration of the perils of deceit afforded to a youngster who was at an age best suited to receive such impressions. That he should exhaust the resources of a youthful but powerful vocabulary upon the crew in general, and Sam in particular, was only to be expected. They bore him no malice for it, but, when he showed signs of going beyond his years, held a hasty consultation, and then stopped his mouth with sixpence-halfpenny and a broken jack-knife.

9

THE SKIPPER OF THE 'OSPREY'

It was a quarter to six in the morning as the mate of the sailing-barge Osprey came on deck and looked round for the master, who had been sleeping ashore and was somewhat overdue. Ten minutes passed before he appeared on the wharf, and the mate saw with surprise that he was leaning on the arm of a pretty girl of twenty, as he hobbled painfully down to the barge.

'Here you are then,' said the mate, his face clearing. 'I began to think you weren't coming.'

'I'm not,' said the skipper; 'I've got the gout crool bad. My darter here's going to take my place, an' I'm going to take it easy in bed for a bit.'

'I'll go an' make it for you,' said the mate.

'I mean my bed at home,' said the skipper sharply. 'I want good nursing an' attention.'

The mate looked puzzled.

'But you don't really mean to say this young lady is coming aboard instead of you?' he said.

'That's just what I do mean,' said the skipper. 'She knows as much about it as I do. She lived aboard with me until she was quite a big girl. You'll take your orders from her. What are you whistling about? Can't I do as I like about my own ship?'

'O' course you can,' said the mate drily; 'an' I s'pose I can whistle if I like—I never heard no orders against it.'

'Gimme a kiss, Meg, an' git aboard,' said the skipper, leaning on his stick and turning his cheek to his daughter, who obediently gave him a perfunctory kiss on the left eyebrow, and sprang lightly aboard the barge.

'Cast off,' said she, in a business-like manner, as she seized a boat-hook and pushed off from the jetty. 'Ta ta, Dad, and go straight home, mind; the cab's waiting.'

'Ay, ay, my dear,' said the proud father, his eye moistening with paternal pride as his daughter, throwing off her jacket, ran and assisted the mate with the sail. 'Lord, what a fine boy she would have made!'

He watched the barge until she was well under way, and then, waving his hand to his daughter, crawled slowly back to the cab; and, being to a certain extent a believer in homeopathy, treated his complaint with a glass of rum.

'I'm sorry your father's so bad, miss,' said the mate, who was still somewhat dazed by the recent proceedings, as the girl came up and took the wheel from him. 'He was complaining a goodish bit all the way up.'

'A wilful man must have his way,' said Miss Cringle, with a shake of her head. 'It's no good me saying anything, because directly my back's turned he has his own way again.'

The mate shook his head despondently.

'You'd better get your bedding up and make your arrangements forward,' said the new skipper presently. There was a look of indulgent admiration in the mate's eye, and she thought it necessary to check it.

'All right,' said the other, 'plenty of time for that; the river's a little bit thick just now.'

'What do you mean?' inquired the girl hastily.

'Some o' these things are not so careful as they might be,'

said the mate, noting the ominous sparkle of her eye, 'an' they might scrape the paint off.'

'Look here, my lad,' said the new skipper grimly, 'if you think you can steer better than me, you'd better keep it to yourself, that's all. Now suppose you see about your bedding, as I said.'

The mate went, albeit he was rather surprised at himself for doing so, and hid his annoyance and confusion beneath the mattress which he brought up on his head. His job completed, he came aft again, and, sitting on the hatches, lit his pipe.

'This is just the weather for a pleasant cruise,' he said amiably, after a few whiffs. 'You've chose a nice time for it.'

'I don't mind the weather,' said the girl, who fancied that there was a little latent sarcasm somewhere. 'I think you'd better wash the decks now.'

'Washed 'em last night,' said the mate, without moving.

'Ah, after dark, perhaps,' said the girl. 'Well, I think I'll have them done again.'

The mate sat pondering rebelliously for a few minutes, then he removed his jacket, put on in honour of the new skipper, and, fetching the bucket and mop, silently obeyed orders.

'You seem to be very fond of sitting down,' remarked the girl, after he had finished; 'can't you find something else to do?'

'I don't know,' replied the mate slowly; 'I thought you were looking after that.'

The girl bit her lip, and was looking carefully round her, when they were both disturbed by the unseemly behaviour of the master of a passing craft.

'Jack!' he yelled in a tone of strong amazement, 'Jack!'

'Halloa!' cried the mate.

'Why didn't you tell us?' yelled the other reproachfully.

'Tell you what?' roared the mystified mate.

The master of the other craft, holding on to the stays with

one hand, jerked his thumb expressively towards Miss Cringle, and waited.

'When was it?' he screamed anxiously, as he realised that his craft was rapidly carrying him out of earshot.

The mate smiled feebly, and glanced uneasily at the girl, who, with a fine colour and an air of vast unconcern, was looking straight in front of her; and it was a relief to both of them when they found themselves hesitating and dodging in front of a schooner which was coming up.

'Do you want all the river?' demanded the exasperated master of the latter vessel, running to the side as they passed. 'Why don't you drop anchor if you want to spoon?'

'Perhaps you'd better let me take the wheel a bit,' said the mate, not without a little malice in his voice.

'No; you can go an' keep a look-out in the bows,' said the girl serenely. 'It'll prevent misunderstandings, too. Better take the potatoes with you and peel them for dinner.'

The mate complied, and the voyage proceeded in silence, the steering being rendered a little nicer than usual by various nautical sparks bringing their boats a bit closer than was necessary in order to obtain a good view of the fair steersman.

After dinner, the tide having turned and a stiff head-wind blowing, they brought up off Sheppey. It began to rain hard, and the crew of the Osprey, having made all snug above, retired to the cabin to resume their quarrel.

'Don't mind me,' said Miss Cringle scathingly, as the mate lit his pipe.

'Well, I didn't think you minded,' replied the mate; 'the old man—'

'Who?' interrupted Miss Cringle, in a tone of polite inquiry.

'Captain Cringle,' said the mate, correcting himself, 'smokes a great deal, and I've heard him say that you liked the smell of it.'

'There's pipes and pipes,' said Miss Cringle oracularly.

The mate flung his on the floor and crunched it beneath his heel, then he thrust his hands in his pockets, and, leaning back, scowled darkly up at the rain as it crackled on the skylight.

'If you are going to show off your nasty temper,' said the girl severely, 'you'd better go forward. It's not quite the thing after all for you to be down here—not that I study appearances much.'

'I shouldn't think you did,' retorted the mate, whose temper was rapidly getting the better of him. 'I can't think what your father was thinking of to let a pret—to let a girl like you come away like this.'

'If you were going to say pretty girl,' said Miss Cringle, with calm self-abnegation, 'don't mind me, say it. The captain knows what he's about. He told me you were a milksop; he said you were a good young man and a teetotaller.'

The mate, allowing the truth of the captain's statement as to his abstinence, hotly denied the charge of goodness. 'I can understand your father's hurry to get rid of you for a spell,' he concluded, being goaded beyond all consideration of politeness. 'His gout 'ud never get well while you were with him. More than that, I shouldn't wonder if you were the cause of it.'

With this parting shot he departed, before the girl could think of a suitable reply, and went and sulked in the dingy little fo'c'sle.

In the evening, the weather having moderated somewhat, and the tide being on the ebb, they got under way again, the girl coming on deck fully attired in an oilskin coat and sou'-wester to resume the command. The rain fell steadily as they ploughed along their way, guided by the bright eye of the 'Mouse' as it shone across the darkening waters. The mate, soaked to the skin, was at the wheel.

'Why don't you go below and put your oilskins on?' inquired

the girl, when this fact dawned upon her.

'Don't want 'em,' said the mate.

'I suppose you know best,' said the girl, and said no more until nine o'clock, when she paused at the companion to give her last orders for the night.

'I'm going to turn in,' said she; 'call me at two o'clock. Good-night.'

'Good-night,' said the other, and the girl vanished.

Left to himself, the mate, who began to feel chilly, felt in his pockets for a pipe, and was in all the stress of getting a light, when he heard a thin, almost mild voice behind him, and, looking round, saw the face of the girl at the companion.

'I say, are these your oilskins I've been wearing?' she demanded awkwardly.

'You're quite welcome,' said the mate.

'Why didn't you tell me?' said the girl indignantly. 'I wouldn't have worn them for anything if I had known it.'

'Well, they won't poison you,' said the mate resentfully. 'Your father left his at Ipswich to have 'em cobbled up a bit.'

The girl passed them up on the deck, and, closing the companion with a bang, disappeared. It is possible that the fatigues of the day had been too much for her, for when she awoke, and consulted the little silver watch that hung by her bunk, it was past five o'clock, and the red glow of the sun was flooding the cabin as she arose and hastily dressed.

The deck was drying in white patches as she went above, and the mate was sitting yawning at the wheel, his eyelids red for want of sleep.

'Didn't I tell you to call me at two o'clock?' she demanded, confronting him.

'It's all right,' said the mate. 'I thought when you woke would be soon enough. You looked tired.'

'I think you'd better go when we get to Ipswich,' said the

girl, tightening her lips. 'I'll ship somebody who'll obey orders.'

'I'll go when we get back to London,' said the mate. 'I'll hand this barge over to the cap'n, and nobody else.'

'Well, we'll see,' said the girl, as she took the wheel, 'I think you'll go at Ipswich.'

For the remainder of the voyage the subject was not alluded to; the mate, in a spirit of sulky pride, kept to the fore part of the boat, except when he was steering, and, as far as practicable, the girl ignored his presence. In this spirit of mutual forbearance they entered the Orwell, and ran swiftly up to Ipswich.

It was late in the afternoon when they arrived there, and the new skipper, waiting only until they were made fast, went ashore, leaving the mate in charge. She had been gone about an hour when a small telegraph boy appeared, and, after boarding the barge in the unsafest manner possible, handed him a telegram. The mate read it and his face flushed. With even more than the curtness customary in language at a halfpenny a word, it contained his dismissal.

'I've had a telegram from your father sacking me,' he said to the girl, as she returned soon after, laden with small parcels.

'Yes, I wired him to,' she replied calmly. 'I suppose you'll go NOW?'

'I'd rather go back to London with you,' he said slowly.

'I daresay,' said the girl. 'As a matter of fact I wasn't really meaning for you to go, but when you said you wouldn't I thought we'd see who was master. I've shipped another mate, so you see I haven't lost much time.'

'Who is he,' inquired the mate.

'Man named Charlie Lee,' replied the girl; 'the foreman here told me of him.'

'He'd no business too,' said the mate, frowning; 'he's a loose fish; take my advice now and ship somebody else. He's not at all the sort of chap I'd choose for you to sail with.'

'You'd choose,' said the girl scornfully; 'dear me, what a pity you didn't tell me before.'

'He's a public-house loafer,' said the mate, meeting her eye angrily, 'and about as bad as they make 'em; but I s'pose you'll have your own way.'

'He won't frighten me,' said the girl. 'I'm quite capable of taking care of myself, thank you. Good evening.'

The mate stepped ashore with a small bundle, leaving the remainder of his possessions to go back to London with the barge. The girl watched his well-knit figure as it strode up the quay until it was out of sight, and then, inwardly piqued because he had not turned round for a parting glance, gave a little sigh, and went below to tea.

The docile and respectful behaviour of the new-comer was a pleasant change to the autocrat of the Osprey, and cargoes were worked out and in without an unpleasant word. They laid at the quay for two days, the new mate, whose home was at Ipswich, sleeping ashore, and on the morning of the third he turned up punctually at six o'clock, and they started on their return voyage.

'Well, you do know how to handle a craft,' said Lee admiringly, as they passed down the river. 'The old boat seems to know it's got a pretty young lady in charge.'

'Don't talk rubbish,' said the girl austerely.

The new mate carefully adjusted his red necktie and smiled indulgently.

'Well, you're the prettiest cap'n I've ever sailed under,' he said. 'What do they call that red cap you've got on? Tam-o'-Shanter is it?'

'I don't know,' said the girl shortly.

'You mean you won't tell me,' said the other, with a look of anger in his soft dark eyes.

'Just as you like,' said she, and Lee, whistling softly, turned on his heel and began to busy himself with some small matter forward.

The rest of the day passed quietly, though there was a freedom in the new mate's manner which made the redoubtable skipper of the Osprey regret her change of crew, and to treat him with more civility than her proud spirit quite approved of. There was but little wind, and the barge merely crawled along as the captain and mate, with surreptitious glances, took each other's measure.

'This is the nicest trip I've ever had,' said Lee, as he came up from an unduly prolonged tea, with a strong-smelling cigar in his mouth. 'I've brought your jacket up.'

'I don't want it, thank you,' said the girl.

'Better have it,' said Lee, holding it up for her.

'When I want my jacket I'll put it on myself,' said the girl.

'All right, no offence,' said the other airily. 'What an obstinate little devil you are.'

'Have you got any drink down there?' inquired the girl, eyeing him sternly.

'Just a little drop o' whiskey, my dear, for the spasms,' said Lee facetiously. 'Will you have a drop?'

'I won't have any drinking here,' said she sharply. 'If you want to drink, wait till you get ashore.'

'YOU won't have any drinking!' said the other, opening his eyes, and with a quiet chuckle he dived below and brought up a bottle and a glass. 'Here's wishing a better temper to you, my dear,' he said amiably, as he tossed off a glass. 'Come, you'd better have a drop. It'll put a little colour in your cheeks.'

'Put it away now, there's a good fellow,' said the captain timidly, as she looked anxiously at the nearest sail, some two miles distant.

'It's the only friend I've got,' said Lee, sprawling gracefully on the hatches, and replenishing his glass. 'Look here. Are you on for a bargain?'

'What do you mean?' inquired the girl.

'Give me a kiss, little spitfire, and I won't take another drop to-night,' said the new mate tenderly. 'Come, I won't tell.'

'You may drink yourself to death before I'll do that,' said the girl, striving to speak calmly. 'Don't talk that nonsense to me again.'

She stooped over as she spoke and made a sudden grab at the bottle, but the new mate was too quick for her, and, snatching it up jeeringly, dared her to come for it.

'Come on, come and fight for it,' said he; 'hit me if you like, I don't mind; your little fist won't hurt.'

No answer being vouchsafed to this invitation he applied himself to his only friend again, while the girl, now thoroughly frightened, steered in silence.

'Better get the sidelights out,' said she at length.

'Plenty o' time,' said Lee.

'Take the helm, then, while I do it,' said the girl, biting her lips.

The fellow rose and came towards her, and, as she made way for him, threw his arm round her waist and tried to detain her. Her heart beating quickly, she walked forward, and, not without a hesitating glance at the drunken figure at the wheel, descended into the fo'c'sle for the lamps.

The next moment, with a gasping little cry, she sank down on a locker as the dark figure of a man rose and stood by her.

'Don't be frightened,' it said quietly.

'Jack?' said the girl.

'That's me,' said the figure. 'You didn't expect to see me, did you? I thought perhaps you didn't know what was good for you, so I stowed myself away last night, and here I am.'

'Have you heard what that fellow has been saying to me?' demanded Miss Cringle, with a spice of the old temper leavening her voice once more.

'Every word,' said the mate cheerfully.

'Why didn't you come up and stand by me?' inquired the girl hotly.

The mate hung his head.

'Oh,' said the girl, and her tones were those of acute disappointment, 'you're afraid.'

'I'm not,' said the mate scornfully.

'Why didn't you come up, then, instead of skulking down here?' inquired the girl.

The mate scratched the back of his neck and smiled, but weakly. 'Well, I—I thought—' he began, and stopped.

'You thought—' prompted Miss Cringle coldly.

'I thought a little fright would do you good,' said the mate, speaking quickly, 'and that it would make you appreciate me a little more when I did come.'

'Ahoy! MAGGIE! MAGGIE!' came the voice of the graceless varlet who was steering.

'I'll MAGGIE him,' said the mate, grinding his teeth, 'Why, what the—why you're crying.'

'I'm not,' sobbed Miss Cringle scornfully. 'I'm in a temper, that's all.'

'I'll knock his head off,' said the mate; 'you stay down here.'

'Mag-GIE!' came the voice again, 'MAG—HULLO!'

'Were you calling me, my lad?' said the mate, with dangerous politeness, as he stepped aft. 'Ain't you afraid of straining that sweet voice o' yours? Leave go o' that tiller.'

The other let go, and the mate's fist took him heavily in the face and sent him sprawling on the deck. He rose with a scream of rage and rushed at his opponent, but the mate's temper, which had suffered badly through his treatment of the last few days, was up, and he sent him heavily down again.

'There's a little dark dingy hole forward,' said the mate,

after waiting some time for him to rise again, 'just the place for you to go and think over your sins in. If I see you come out of it until we get to London, I'll hurt you. Now clear.'

The other cleared, and, carefully avoiding the girl, who was standing close by, disappeared below.

'You've hurt him,' said the girl, coming up to the mate and laying her hand on his arm. 'What a horrid temper you've got.'

'It was him asking you to kiss him that upset me,' said the mate apologetically.

'He put his arm round my waist,' said Miss Cringle, blushing.

'WHAT!' said the mate, stuttering, 'put his—put his arm—round—your waist—like—'

His courage suddenly forsook him.

'Like what?' inquired the girl, with superb innocence.

'Like THAT,' said the mate manfully.

'That'll do,' said Miss Cringle softly, 'that'll do. You're as bad as he is, only the worst of it is there is nobody here to prevent you.'

10

A GOLDEN VENTURE

The elders of the Tidger family sat at breakfast—Mrs Tidger with knees wide apart and the youngest Tidger nestling in the valley of a print-dress which lay between, and Mr Tidger bearing on one moleskin knee a small copy of himself in a red flannel frock and a slipper. The larger Tidger children took the solids of their breakfast up and down the stone-flagged court outside, coming in occasionally to gulp draughts of very weak tea from a gallipot or two which stood on the table, and to wheedle Mr Tidger out of any small piece of bloater which he felt generous enough to bestow.

'Peg away, Ann,' said Mr Tidger, heartily. His wife's elder sister shook her head, and passing the remains of her slice to one of her small nephews, leaned back in her chair. 'No appetite, Tidger,' she said, slowly. 'You should go in for carpentering,' said Mr Tidger, in justification of the huge crust he was carving into mouthfuls with his pocket-knife. 'Seems to me I can't eat enough sometimes. Hullo, who's the letter for?' He took it from the postman, who stood at the door amid a bevy of Tidgers who had followed him up the court, and slowly read the address. 'Mrs Ann Pullen,' he said, handing it over to his sister-in-law; 'nice writing, too.' Mrs Pullen broke the envelope, and after a somewhat lengthy search for her pocket, fumbled therein for her spectacles. She then searched the mantelpiece, the chest of drawers, and the dresser, and finally ran them to earth on the copper.

She was not a good scholar, and it took her some time to read the letter, a proceeding which she punctuated with such 'Ohs' and 'Ahs' and gaspings and 'God bless my souls' as nearly drove the carpenter and his wife, who were leaning forward impatiently, to the verge of desperation.

'Who's it from?' asked Mr Tidger for the third time.

'I don't know,' said Mrs Pullen. 'Good gracious, who ever would ha' thought it!'

'Thought what, Ann?' demanded the carpenter, feverishly.

'Why don't people write their names plain?' demanded his sister-in-law, impatiently. 'It's got a printed name up in the corner; perhaps that's it. Well, I never did—I don't know whether I'm standing on my head or my heels.'

'You're sitting down, that's what you're a-doing,' said the carpenter, regarding her somewhat unfavourably.

'Perhaps it's a take-in,' said Mrs Pullen, her lips trembling. 'I've heard o' such things. If it is, I shall never get over it—never.'

'Get—over—what?' asked the carpenter.

'It don't look like a take-in,' soliloquized Mrs Pullen, 'and I shouldn't think anybody'd go to all that trouble and spend a penny to take in a poor thing like me.'

Mr Tidger, throwing politeness to the winds, leaped forward, and snatching the letter from her, read it with feverish haste, tempered by a defective education.

'It's a take-in, Ann,' he said, his voice trembling; 'it must be.'

'What is?' asked Mrs Tidger, impatiently.

'Looks like it,' said Mrs Pullen, feebly.

'What is it?' screamed Mrs Tidger, wrought beyond all

endurance.

Her husband turned and regarded her with much severity, but Mrs Tidger's gaze was the stronger, and after a vain attempt to meet it, he handed her the letter.

Mrs Tidger read it through hastily, and then snatching the baby from her lap, held it out with both arms to her husband, and jumping up, kissed her sister heartily, patting her on the back in her excitement until she coughed with the pain of it.

'You don't think it's a take-in, Polly?' she inquired.

'Take-in?' said her sister; 'of course it ain't. Lawyers don't play jokes; their time's too valuable. No, you're an heiress all right, Ann, and I wish you joy. I couldn't be more pleased if it was myself.'

She kissed her again, and going to pat her back once more, discovered that she had sunk down sufficiently low in her chair to obtain the protection of its back.

'Two thousand pounds,' said Mrs Pullen, in an awestruck voice.

'Ten hundred pounds twice over,' said the carpenter, mouthing it slowly; 'twenty hundred pounds.'

He got up from the table, and instinctively realizing that he could not do full justice to his feelings with the baby in his arms, laid it on the teatray in a puddle of cold tea and stood looking hard at the heiress.

'I was housekeeper to her eleven years ago,' said Mrs Pullen. 'I wonder what she left it to me for?'

'Didn't know what to do with it, I should think,' said the carpenter, still staring open-mouthed.

'Tidger, I'm ashamed of you,' said his wife, snatching her infant to her bosom. 'I expect you was very good to her, Ann.'

'I never 'ad no luck,' said the impenitent carpenter. 'Nobody ever left me no money. Nobody ever left me so much as a fi-pun note.'

He stared round disdainfully at his poor belongings, and drawing on his coat, took his bag from a corner, and hoisting it on his shoulder, started to his work. He scattered the news as he went, and it ran up and down the little main street of Thatcham, and thence to the outlying lanes and cottages. Within a couple of hours it was common property, and the fortunate legatee was presented with a congratulatory address every time she ventured near the door.

It is an old adage that money makes friends; the carpenter was surprised to find that the mere fact of his having a moneyed relation had the same effect, and that men to whom he had hitherto shown a certain amount of respect due to their position now sought his company. They stood him beer at the 'Bell,' and walked by his side through the street. When they took to dropping in of an evening to smoke a pipe the carpenter was radiant with happiness.

'You don't seem to see beyond the end of your nose, Tidger,' said the wife of his bosom after they had retired one evening.

'H'm?' said the startled carpenter.

'What do you think old Miller, the dealer, comes here for?' demanded his wife.

'Smoke his pipe,' replied her husband, confidently.

'And old Wiggett?' persisted Mrs Tidger.

'Smoke his pipe,' was the reply. 'Why, what's the matter, Polly?'

Mrs Tidger sniffed derisively. 'You men are all alike,' she snapped. 'What do you think Ann wears that pink bodice for?'

'I never noticed she 'ad a pink bodice, Polly,' said the carpenter.

'No? That's what I say. You men never notice anything,' said his wife. 'If you don't send them two old fools off, I will.'

'Don't you like 'em to see Ann wearing pink?' inquired the mystified Tidger.

Mrs Tidger bit her lip and shook her head at him scornfully. 'In plain English, Tidger, as plain as I can speak it,'—she said, severely, 'they're after Ann and 'er bit o' money.'

Mr Tidger gazed at her open-mouthed, and taking advantage of that fact, blew out the candle to hide his discomposure. 'What!' he said, blankly, 'at 'er time o' life?'

'Watch 'em to-morrer,' said his wife.

The carpenter acted upon his instructions, and his ire rose as he noticed the assiduous attention paid by his two friends to the frivolous Mrs Pullen. Mr Wiggett, a sharp-featured little man, was doing most of the talking, while his rival, a stout, clean-shaven man with a slow, ox-like eye, looked on stolidly. Mr Miller was seldom in a hurry, and lost many a bargain through his slowness—a fact which sometimes so painfully affected the individual who had outdistanced him that he would offer to let him have it at a still lower figure.

'You get younger than ever, Mrs Pullen,' said Wiggett, the conversation having turned upon ages.

'Young ain't the word for it,' said Miller, with a praiseworthy determination not to be left behind.

'No; it's age as you're thinking of, Mr Wiggett,' said the carpenter, slowly; 'none of us gets younger, do we, Ann?'

'Some of us keeps young in our ways,' said Mrs Pullen, somewhat shortly.

'How old should you say Ann is now?' persisted the watchful Tidger.

Mr Wiggett shook his head. 'I should say she's about fifteen years younger nor me,' he said, slowly, 'and I'm as lively as a cricket.'

'She's fifty-five,' said the carpenter.

'That makes you seventy, Wiggett,' said Mr Miller, pointedly. 'I thought you was more than that. You look it.'

Mr Wiggett coughed sourly. 'I'm fifty-nine,' he growled.

'Nothing'll make me believe as Mrs Pullen's fifty-five, nor anywhere near it.'

'Ho!' said the carpenter, on his mettle—'ho! Why, my wife here was the sixth child, and she—' He caught a gleam in the sixth child's eye, and expressed her age with a cough. The others waited politely until he had finished, and Mr Tidger, noticing this, coughed again.

'And she—' prompted Mr Miller, displaying a polite interest.

'She ain't so young as she was,' said the carpenter.

'Cares of a family,' said Mr Wiggett, plumping boldly. 'I always thought Mrs Pullen was younger than her.'

'So did I,' said Mr Miller, 'much younger.'

Mr Wiggett eyed him sharply. It was rather hard to have Miller hiding his lack of invention by participating in his compliments and even improving upon them. It was the way he dealt at market-listening to other dealers' accounts of their wares, and adding to them for his own.

'I was noticing you the other day, ma'am,' continued Mr Wiggett. 'I see you going up the road with a step free and easy as a young girl's.'

'She allus walks like that,' said Mr Miller, in a tone of surprised reproof.

'It's in the family,' said the carpenter, who had been uneasily watching his wife's face.

'Both of you seem to notice a lot,' said Mrs Tidger; 'much more than you used to.'

Mr Tidger, who was of a nervous and sensitive disposition, coughed again.

'You ought to take something for that cough,' said Mr Wiggett, considerately.

'Gin and beer,' said Mr Miller, with the air of a specialist.

'Bed's the best thing for it,' said Mrs Tidger, whose temper was beginning to show signs of getting out of hand.

Mr Tidger rose and looked awkwardly at his visitors; Mr Wiggett got up, and pretending to notice the time, said he must be going, and looked at Mr Miller. That gentleman, who was apparently deep in some knotty problem, was gazing at the floor, and oblivious for the time to his surroundings.

'Come along,' said Wiggett, with feigned heartiness, slapping him on the back.

Mr Miller, looking for a moment as though he would like to return the compliment, came back to everyday life, and bidding the company good-night, stepped to the door, accompanied by his rival. It was immediately shut with some violence.

'They seem in a hurry,' said Wiggett. 'I don't think I shall go there again.'

'I don't think I shall,' said Mr Miller.

After this neither of them was surprised to meet there again the next night, and indeed for several nights. The carpenter and his wife, who did not want the money to go out of the family, and were also afraid of offending Mrs Pullen, were at their wits' end what to do. Ultimately it was resolved that Tidger, in as delicate a manner as possible, was to hint to her that they were after her money. He was so vague and so delicate that Mrs Pullen misunderstood him, and fancying that he was trying to borrow half a crown, made him a present of five shillings.

It was evident to the slower-going Mr Miller that his rival's tongue was giving him an advantage which only the ever-watchful presence of the carpenter and his wife prevented him from pushing to the fullest advantage. In these circumstances he sat for two hours after breakfast one morning in deep cogitation, and after six pipes got up with a twinkle in his slow eyes which his brother dealers had got to regard as a danger signal.

He had only the glimmering of an idea at first, but after a couple of pints at the 'Bell' everything took shape, and he cast his eyes about for an assistant. They fell upon a man named Smith, and the dealer, after some thought, took up his glass and went over to him.

'I want you to do something for me,' he remarked, in a mysterious voice.

'Ah, I've been wanting to see you,' said Smith, who was also a dealer in a small way. 'One o' them hins I bought off you last week is dead.'

'I'll give you another for it,' said Miller.

'And the others are so forgetful,' continued Mr Smith.

'Forgetful?' repeated the other.

'Forget to lay, like,' said Mr Smith, musingly.

'Never mind about them,' said Mr Miller, with some animation. 'I want you to do something for me. If it comes off all right, I'll give you a dozen hins and a couple of decentish-sized pigs.'

Mr Smith called a halt. 'Decentish-sized' was vague.

'Take your pick,' said Mr Miller. 'You know Mrs Pullen's got two thousand pounds—'

'Wiggett's going to have it,' said the other; 'he as good as told me so.'

'He's after her money,' said the other, sadly. 'Look 'ere, Smith, I want you to tell him she's lost it all. Say that Tidger told you, but you wasn't to tell anybody else. Wiggett'll believe you.'

Mr Smith turned upon him a face all wrinkles, lit by one eye. 'I want the hins and the pigs first,' he said, firmly.

Mr Miller, shocked at his grasping spirit, stared at him mournfully.

'And twenty pounds the day you marry Mrs Pullen,' continued Mr Smith.

Mr Miller, leading him up and down the sawdust floor, besought him to listen to reason, and Mr Smith allowed the better feelings of our common human nature to prevail to the extent of reducing his demands to half a dozen fowls on account, and all the rest on the day of the marriage. Then, with the delightful feeling that he wouldn't do any work for a week, he went out to drop poison into the ears of Mr Wiggett.

'Lost all her money!' said the startled Mr Wiggett. 'How?'

'I don't know how,' said his friend. 'Tidger told me, but made me promise not to tell a soul. But I couldn't help telling you, Wiggett, 'cause I know what you're after.'

'Do me a favour,' said the little man.

'I will,' said the other.

'Keep it from Miller as long as possible. If you hear any one else talking of it, tell 'em to keep it from him. If he marries her I'll give you a couple of pints.'

Mr Smith promised faithfully, and both the Tidgers and Mrs Pullen were surprised to find that Mr Miller was the only visitor that evening. He spoke but little, and that little in a slow, ponderous voice intended for Mrs Pullen's ear alone. He spoke disparagingly of money, and shook his head slowly at the temptations it brought in its train. Give him a crust, he said, and somebody to halve it with—a home-made crust baked by a wife. It was a pretty picture, but somewhat spoiled by Mrs Tidger suggesting that, though he had spoken of halving the crust, he had said nothing about the beer.

'Half of my beer wouldn't be much,' said the dealer, slowly.

'Not the half you would give your wife wouldn't,' retorted Mrs Tidger.

The dealer sighed and looked mournfully at Mrs Pullen. The lady sighed in return, and finding that her admirer's stock of conversation seemed to be exhausted, coyly suggested a game of draughts. The dealer assented with eagerness, and declining the offer of a glass of beer by explaining that he had had one the day before yesterday, sat down and lost seven games right off. He gave up at the seventh game, and pushing back his chair, said that he thought Mrs Pullen was the most wonderful draught-player he had ever seen, and took no notice when Mrs Tidger, in a dry voice charged with subtle meaning, said that she thought he was.

'Draughts come natural to some people,' said Mrs Pullen, modestly. 'It's as easy as kissing your fingers.'

Mr Miller looked doubtful; then he put his great fingers to his lips by way of experiment, and let them fall unmistakably in the widow's direction. Mrs Pullen looked down and nearly blushed. The carpenter and his wife eyed each other in indignant consternation.

'That's easy enough,' said the dealer, and repeated the offense.

Mrs Pullen got up in some confusion, and began to put the draught-board away. One of the pieces fell on the floor, and as they both stooped to recover it their heads bumped. It was nothing to the dealer's, but Mrs Pullen rubbed hers and sat down with her eyes watering. Mr Miller took out his handkerchief, and going to the scullery, dipped it into water and held it to her head.

'Is it better?' he inquired.

'A little better,' said the victim, with a shiver.

Mr Miller, in his emotion, was squeezing the handkerchief hard, and a cold stream was running down her neck.

'Thank you. It's all right now.'

The dealer replaced the handkerchief, and sat for some time regarding her earnestly. Then the carpenter and his wife displaying manifest signs of impatience, he took his departure, after first inviting himself for another game of draughts the following night.

He walked home with the air of a conqueror, and thought exultingly that the two thousand pounds were his. It was a deal after his own heart, and not the least satisfactory part about it was the way he had got the better of Wiggett.

He completed his scheme the following day after a short interview with the useful Smith. By the afternoon Wiggett found that his exclusive information was common property, and all Thatcham was marvelling at the fortitude with which Mrs Pullen was bearing the loss of her fortune. With a view of being out of the way when the denial was published, Mr Miller, after loudly expressing in public his sympathy for Mrs Pullen and his admiration of her qualities, drove over with some pigs to a neighbouring village, returning to Thatcham in the early evening. Then hurriedly putting his horse up he made his way to the carpenter's.

The Tidgers were at home when he entered, and Mrs Pullen flushed faintly as he shook hands.

'I was coming in before,' he said, impressively, 'after what I heard this afternoon, but I had to drive over to Thorpe.'

'You 'eard it?' inquired the carpenter, in an incredulous voice.

'Certainly,' said the dealer, 'and very sorry I was. Sorry for one thing, but glad for another.'

The carpenter opened his mouth and seemed about to speak. Then he checked himself suddenly and gazed with interest at the ingenuous dealer.

'I'm glad,' said Mr Miller, slowly, as he nodded at a friend of Mrs Tidger's who had just come in with a long face, 'because now that Mrs Pullen is poor, I can say to her what I couldn't say while she was rich.'

Again the astonished carpenter was about to speak, but the dealer hastily checked him with his hand.

'One at a time,' he said. 'Mrs Pullen, I was very sorry to hear this afternoon, for your sake, that you had lost all your money. What I wanted to say to you now, now that you are poor, was to ask you to be Mrs Miller. What d'ye say?'

Mrs Pullen, touched at so much goodness, wept softly and said, 'Yes.' The triumphant Miller took out his handkerchief—the same that he had used the previous night, for he was not an extravagant man—and tenderly wiped her eyes.

'Well, I'm blowed!' said the staring carpenter.

'I've got a nice little 'ouse,' continued the wily Mr Miller. 'It's a poor place, but nice, and we'll play draughts every evening. When shall it be?'

'When you like,' said Mrs Pullen, in a faint voice.

'I'll put the banns up to-morrow,' said the dealer.

Mrs Tidger's lady friend giggled at so much haste, but Mrs Tidger, who felt that she had misjudged him, was touched.

'It does you credit, Mr Miller,' she said, warmly.

'No, no,' said the dealer; and then Mr Tidger got up, and crossing the room, solemnly shook hands with him.

'Money or no money, she'll make a good wife,' he said.

'I'm glad you're pleased,' said the dealer, wondering at this cordiality.

'I don't deny I thought you was after her money,' continued the carpenter, solemnly. 'My missus thought so, too.'

Mr Miller shook his head, and said he thought they would have known him better.

'Of course it is a great loss,' said the carpenter. 'Money is money.'

'That's all it is, though,' said the slightly mystified Mr Miller.

'What I can't understand is,' continued the carpenter, "ow the news got about. Why, the neighbours knew of it a couple of hours before we did.'

The dealer hid a grin. Then he looked a bit bewildered again.

'I assure you,' said the carpenter, 'it was known in the town at least a couple of hours before we got the letter.'

Mr Miller waited a minute to get perfect control over his features. 'Letter?' he repeated, faintly.

'The letter from the lawyers,' said the carpenter.

Mr Miller was silent again. His features were getting tiresome. He eyed the door furtively.

'What-was-in-the letter?' he asked.

'Short and sweet,' said the carpenter, with bitterness. 'Said it was all a mistake, because they'd been and found another will. People shouldn't make such mistakes.'

'We're all liable to make mistakes,' said Miller, thinking he saw an opening.

'Yes, we made a mistake when we thought you was after Ann's money,' assented the carpenter. 'I'm sure I thought you'd be the last man in the world to be pleased to hear that she'd lost it. One thing is, you've got enough for both.'

Mr Miller made no reply, but in a dazed way strove to realize the full measure of the misfortune which had befallen him. The neighbour, with the anxiety of her sex to be the first with a bit of news, had already taken her departure. He thought of Wiggett walking the earth a free man, and of Smith with a three-months' bill for twenty pounds. His pride as a dealer was shattered beyond repair, and emerging from a species of mist, he became conscious that the carpenter was addressing him.

'We'll leave you two young things alone for a bit,' said Mr Tidger, heartily. 'We're going out. When you're tired o' courting you can play draughts, and Ann will show you one or two of 'er moves. So long.'

11

BILL'S PAPER CHASE

Sailormen 'ave their faults, said the night watchman, frankly. I'm not denying of it. I used to 'ave myself when I was at sea, but being close with their money is a fault as can seldom be brought ag'in 'em.

I saved some money once—two golden sovereigns, owing to a 'ole in my pocket. Before I got another ship I slept two nights on a doorstep and 'ad nothing to eat, and I found them two sovereigns in the lining o' my coat when I was over two thousand miles away from the nearest pub.

I on'y knew one miser all the years I was at sea. Thomas Geary 'is name was, and we was shipmates aboard the barque Grenada, homeward bound from Sydney to London.

Thomas was a man that was getting into years; sixty, I think 'e was, and old enough to know better. 'E'd been saving 'ard for over forty years, and as near as we could make out 'e was worth a matter o' six 'undered pounds. He used to be fond o' talking about it, and letting us know how much better off 'e was than any of the rest of us.

We was about a month out from Sydney when old Thomas took sick. Bill Hicks said that it was owing to a ha'penny he couldn't account for; but Walter Jones, whose family was always ill, and thought 'e knew a lot about it, said that 'e knew wot it was, but 'e couldn't remember the name of it, and that when we got to London and Thomas saw a doctor, we should see as 'ow 'e was right.

Whatever it was the old man got worse and worse. The skipper came down and gave 'im some physic and looked at 'is tongue, and then 'e looked at our tongues to see wot the difference was. Then 'e left the cook in charge of 'im and went off.

The next day Thomas was worse, and it was soon clear to everybody but 'im that 'e was slipping 'is cable. He wouldn't believe it at first, though the cook told 'im, Bill Hicks told him, and Walter Jones 'ad a grandfather that went off in just the same way.

'I'm not going to die,' says Thomas. 'How can I die and leave all that money?'

'It'll be good for your relations, Thomas,' says Walter Jones.

'I ain't got any,' says the old man.

'Well, your friends, then, Thomas,' says Walter, soft-like.

'Ain't got any,' says the old man ag'in.

'Yes, you 'ave, Thomas,' says Walter, with a kind smile; 'I could tell you one you've got.'

Thomas shut his eyes at 'im and began to talk pitiful about 'is money and the 'ard work 'e'd 'ad saving of it. And by-and-by 'e got worse, and didn't reckernise us, but thought we was a pack o' greedy, drunken sailormen. He thought Walter Jones was a shark, and told 'im so, and, try all 'e could, Walter couldn't persuade 'im different.

He died the day arter. In the morning 'e was whimpering about 'is money ag'in, and angry with Bill when 'e reminded 'im that 'e couldn't take it with 'im, and 'e made Bill promise that 'e should be buried just as 'e was. Bill tucked him up arter that, and when 'e felt a canvas belt tied round the old man's waist 'e began to see wot 'e was driving at.

The weather was dirty that day and there was a bit o' sea running, consequently all 'ands was on deck, and a boy about sixteen wot used to 'elp the steward down aft was lookin' arter Thomas. Me and Bill just run down to give a look at the old man in time.

'I am going to take it with me, Bill,' says the old man.

'That's right,' says Bill.

'My mind's—easy now,' says Thomas. 'I gave it to Jimmy—to—to—throw overboard for me.'

'Wot?' says Bill, staring.

'That's right, Bill,' says the boy. 'He told me to. It was a little packet o' banknotes. He gave me tuppence for doing it.'

Old Thomas seemed to be listening. 'Is eyes was open, and 'e looked artful at Bill to think what a clever thing 'e'd done.

'Nobody's goin' to spend my money,' 'e says. 'Nobody's.'

We drew back from 'is bunk and stood staring at 'im. Then Bill turned to the boy.

'Go and tell the skipper 'e's gone,' 'e says, 'and mind, for your own sake, don't tell the skipper or anybody else that you've thrown all that money overboard.'

'Why not?' says Jimmy.

'Becos you'll be locked up for it,' says Bill; 'you'd no business to do it. You've been and broke the law. It ought to ha' been left to somebody.'

Jimmy looked scared, and arter 'e was gone I turned to Bill, and I looks at 'im and I says 'What's the little game, Bill?'

'Game?' said Bill, snorting at me. 'I don't want the pore boy to get into trouble, do I? Pore little chap. You was young yourself once.'

'Yes,' I says; 'but I'm a bit older now, Bill, and unless you tell me what your little game is, I shall tell the skipper myself, and the chaps too. Pore old Thomas told 'im to do it, so where's the boy to blame?'

'Do you think Jimmy did?' says Bill, screwing up his nose at me. 'That little varmint is walking about worth six 'undered quid. Now you keep your mouth shut and I'll make it worth your while.'

Then I see Bill's game. 'All right, I'll keep quiet for the sake of my half,' I says, looking at 'im.

I thought he'd ha' choked, and the langwidge 'e see fit to use was a'most as much as I could answer.

'Very well, then,' 'e says, at last, 'halves it is. It ain't robbery becos it belongs to nobody, and it ain't the boy's becos 'e was told to throw it overboard.'

They buried pore old Thomas next morning, and arter it was all over Bill put 'is 'and on the boy's shoulder as they walked for'ard and 'e says, 'Poor old Thomas 'as gone to look for 'is money,' he says; 'wonder whether 'e'll find it! Was it a big bundle, Jimmy?'

'No,' says the boy, shaking 'is 'ead. 'They was six 'undered pound notes and two sovereigns, and I wrapped the sovereigns up in the notes to make 'em sink. Fancy throwing money away like that, Bill: seems a sin, don't it?'

Bill didn't answer 'im, and that afternoon the other chaps below being asleep we searched 'is bunk through and through without any luck, and at last Bill sat down and swore 'e must ha' got it about 'im.

We waited till night, and when everybody was snoring 'ard we went over to the boy's bunk and went all through 'is pockets and felt the linings, and then we went back to our side and Bill said wot 'e thought about Jimmy in whispers.

'He must ha' got it tied round 'is waist next to 'is skin, like Thomas 'ad,' I says.

We stood there in the dark whispering, and then Bill couldn't stand it any longer, and 'e went over on tiptoe to the bunk ag'in. He was tremblin' with excitement and I wasn't much better, when all of a sudden the cook sat up in 'is bunk with a dreadful laughing scream and called out that somebody was ticklin' 'im.

I got into my bunk and Bill got into 'is, and we lay there listening while the cook, who was a terrible ticklish man, leaned out of 'is bunk and said wot 'e'd do if it 'appened ag'in.

'Go to sleep,' says Walter Jones; 'you're dreamin'. Who d'you think would want to tickle you?'

'I tell you,' says the cook, 'somebody come over and tickled me with a 'and the size of a leg o' mutton. I feel creepy all over.'

Bill gave it up for that night, but the next day 'e pretended to think Jimmy was gettin' fat an' 'e caught 'old of 'im and prodded 'im all over. He thought 'e felt something round 'is waist, but 'e couldn't be sure, and Jimmy made such a noise that the other chaps interfered and told Bill to leave 'im alone. For a whole week we tried to find that money, and couldn't, and Bill said it was a suspicious thing that Jimmy kept aft a good deal more than 'e used to, and 'e got an idea that the boy might ha' 'idden it somewhere there. At the end of that time, 'owever, owing to our being short-'anded, Jimmy was sent for'ard to work as ordinary seaman, and it began to be quite noticeable the way 'e avoided Bill.

At last one day we got 'im alone down the fo'c'sle, and Bill put 'is arm round 'im and got im on the locker and asked 'im straight out where the money was.

'Why, I chucked it overboard,' he says. 'I told you so afore. What a memory you've got, Bill!'

Bill picked 'im up and laid 'im on the locker, and we searched 'im thoroughly. We even took 'is boots off, and then we 'ad another look in 'is bunk while 'e was putting 'em on ag'in.

'If you're innercent,' says Bill, 'why don't you call out?—eh?'

'Because you told me not to say anything about it, Bill,' says the boy. 'But I will next time. Loud, I will.'

'Look 'ere,' says Bill, 'you tell us where it is, and the three of us'll go shares in it. That'll be two 'undered pounds each, and we'll tell you 'ow to get yours changed without getting caught. We're cleverer than you are, you know.'

'I know that, Bill,' says the boy; 'but it's no good me telling you lies. I chucked it overboard.'

'Very good, then,' says Bill, getting up. 'I'm going to tell the skipper.'

'Tell 'im,' says Jimmy. 'I don't care.'

'Then you'll be searched arter you've stepped ashore,' says Bill, 'and you won't be allowed on the ship ag'in. You'll lose it all by being greedy, whereas if you go shares with us you'll 'ave two 'undered pounds.'

I could see as 'ow the boy 'adn't thought o' that, and try as 'e would 'e couldn't 'ide 'is feelin's. He called Bill a red-nosed shark, and 'e called me somethin' I've forgotten now.

'Think it over,' says Bill; 'mind, you'll be collared as soon as you've left the gangway and searched by the police.'

'And will they tickle the cook too, I wonder?' says Jimmy, savagely.

'And if they find it you'll go to prison,' says Bill, giving 'im a clump o' the side o' the 'ead, 'and you won't like that, I can tell you.'

'Why, ain't it nice, Bill?' says Jimmy, holding 'is ear.

Bill looked at 'im and then 'e steps to the ladder. 'I'm not going to talk to you any more, my lad,' 'e says. 'I'm going to tell the skipper.'

He went up slowly, and just as 'e reached the deck Jimmy started up and called 'im. Bill pretended not to 'ear, and the boy ran up on deck and follered 'im; and arter a little while they both came down again together.

'Did you wish to speak to me, my lad?' says Bill, 'olding 'is 'ead up.

'Yes,' says the boy, fiddling with 'is fingers; 'if you keep your ugly mouth shut, we'll go shares.'

'Ho!' says Bill, 'I thought you threw it overboard!'

'I thought so, too, Bill,' says Jimmy, very softly, 'and when I came below ag'in I found it in my trousers pocket.'

'Where is it now?' says Bill.

'Never mind where it is,' says the boy; 'you couldn't get it if I was to tell you. It'll take me all my time to do it myself.'

'Where is it?' says Bill, ag'in. 'I'm goin' to take care of it. I won't trust you.'

'And I can't trust you,' says Jimmy.

'If you don't tell me where it is this minute,' says Bill, moving to the ladder ag'in, 'I'm off to tell the skipper. I want it in my 'ands, or at any rate my share of it. Why not share it out now?'

'Because I 'aven't got it,' says Jimmy, stamping 'is foot, 'that's why, and it's all your silly fault. Arter you came pawing through my pockets when you thought I was asleep I got frightened and 'id it.'

'Where?' says Bill.

'In the second mate's mattress,' says Jimmy. 'I was tidying up down aft and I found a 'ole in the underneath side of 'is mattress and I shoved it in there, and poked it in with a bit o' stick.'

'And 'ow are you going to get it?' says Bill, scratching 'is 'ead.

'That's wot I don't know, seeing that I'm not allowed aft now,' says Jimmy. 'One of us'll 'ave to make a dash for it when we get to London. And mind if there's any 'ankypanky on your part, Bill, I'll give the show away myself.'

The cook came down just then and we 'ad to leave off talking, and I could see that Bill was so pleased at finding that the money 'adn't been thrown overboard that 'e was losing sight o' the difficulty o' getting at it. In a day or two, 'owever, 'e see it as plain as me and Jimmy did, and, as time went by, he got desprit, and frightened us both by 'anging about aft every chance 'e got.

The companion-way faced the wheel, and there was about as much chance o' getting down there without being seen as there would be o' taking a man's false teeth out of 'is mouth without 'is knowing it. Jimmy went down one day while Bill was at the wheel to look for 'is knife, wot 'e thought 'e'd left down there, and 'ed 'ardly got down afore Bill saw 'im come up ag'in, 'olding on to the top of a mop which the steward was using.

We couldn't figure it out nohow, and to think o' the second mate, a little man with a large fam'ly, who never 'ad a penny in 'is pocket, sleeping every night on a six 'undered pound mattress, sent us pretty near crazy. We used to talk it over whenever we got a chance, and Bill and Jimmy could scarcely be civil to each other. The boy said it was Bill's fault, and 'e said it was the boy's.

'The on'y thing I can see,' says the boy, one day, 'is for Bill to 'ave a touch of sunstroke as 'e's leaving the wheel one day, tumble 'ead-first down the companion-way, and injure 'isself so severely that 'e can't be moved. Then they'll put 'im in a cabin down aft, and p'raps I'll 'ave to go and nurse 'im. Anyway, he'll be down there.'

'It's a very good idea, Bill,' I says.

'Ho,' says Bill, looking at me as if 'e would eat me. 'Why don't you do it, then?'

'I'd sooner you did it, Bill,' says the boy; 'still, I don't mind which it is. Why not toss up for it?'

'Get away,' says Bill. 'Get away afore I do something you won't like, you blood-thirsty little murderer.'

'I've got a plan myself,' he says, in a low voice, after the boy 'ad 'opped off, 'and if I can't think of nothing better I'll try it, and mind, not a word to the boy.'

He didn't think o' nothing better, and one night just as we was making the Channel 'e tried 'is plan. He was in the second mate's watch, and by-and-by 'e leans over the wheel and says to 'im in a low voice, 'This is my last v'y'ge, sir.'

'Oh,' says the second mate, who was a man as didn't mind talking to a man before the mast. 'How's that?'

'I've got a berth ashore, sir,' says Bill, 'and I wanted to ask a favour, sir.'

The second mate growled and walked off a pace or two.

'I've never been so 'appy as I've been on this ship,' says Bill; 'none of us 'ave. We was saying so the other night, and everybody agreed as it was owing to you, sir, and your kindness to all of us.'

The second mate coughed, but Bill could see as 'e was a bit pleased.

'The feeling came over me,' says Bill, 'that when I leave the sea for good I'd like to 'ave something o' yours to remember you by, sir. And it seemed to me that if I 'ad your—mattress I should think of you ev'ry night o' my life.'

'My wot?' says the second mate, staring at 'im. 'Your mattress, sir,' says Bill. 'If I might make so bold as to offer a pound for it, sir. I want something wot's been used by you, and I've got a fancy for that as a keepsake.' The second mate shook 'is 'ead. 'I'm sorry, Bill,' 'e says, gently, 'but I couldn't let it go at that.'

'I'd sooner pay thirty shillin's than not 'ave it, sir,' says Bill, 'umbly.

'I gave a lot of money for that mattress,' says the mate, ag'in. 'I forgit 'ow much, but a lot. You don't know 'ow valuable that mattress is.'

'I know it's a good one, sir, else you wouldn't 'ave it,' says Bill. 'Would a couple o' pounds buy it, sir?'

The second mate hum'd and ha'd, but Bill was afeard to go any 'igher. So far as 'e could make out from Jimmy, the mattress was worth about eighteen pence—to anybody who wasn't pertiklar.

'I've slept on that mattress for years,' says the second mate, looking at 'im from the corner of 'is eye. 'I don't believe I could sleep on another. Still, to oblige you, Bill, you shall 'ave it at that if you don't want it till we go ashore?'

'Thankee, sir,' says Bill, 'ardly able to keep from dancing, 'and I'll 'and over the two pounds when we're paid off. I shall keep it all my life, sir, in memory of you and your kindness.'

'And mind you keep quiet about it,' says the second mate, who didn't want the skipper to know wot 'e'd been doing, 'because I don't want to be bothered by other men wanting to buy things as keepsakes.'

Bill promised 'im like a shot, and when 'e told me about it 'e was nearly crying with joy.

'And mind,' 'e says, 'I've bought that mattress, bought it as it stands, and it's got nothing to do with Jimmy. We'll each pay a pound and halve wot's in it.'

He persuaded me at last, but that boy watched us like a cat watching a couple of canaries, and I could see we should 'ave all we could do to deceive 'im. He seemed more suspicious o' Bill than me, and 'e kep' worrying us nearly every day to know what we were going to do.

We beat about in the channel with a strong 'ead-wind for four days, and then a tug picked us up and towed us to London.

The excitement of that last little bit was 'orrible. Fust of all we 'ad got to get the mattress, and then in some way we 'ad got to get rid o' Jimmy. Bill's idea was for me to take 'im ashore with me and tell 'im that Bill would join us arterwards, and then lose 'im; but I said that till I'd got my share I couldn't bear to lose sight o' Bill's honest face for 'alf a second.

And, besides, Jimmy wouldn't 'ave gone.

All the way up the river 'e stuck to Bill, and kept asking 'im wot we were to do. 'E was 'alf crying, and so excited that Bill was afraid the other chaps would notice it.

We got to our berth in the East India Docks at last, and arter we were made fast we went below to 'ave a wash and change into our shoregoing togs. Jimmy watched us all the time, and then 'e comes up to Bill biting 'is nails, and says:

'How's it to be done, Bill?'

'Hang about arter the rest 'ave gone ashore, and trust to luck,' says Bill, looking at me. 'We'll see 'ow the land lays when we draw our advance.'

We went down aft to draw ten shillings each to go ashore with. Bill and me got ours fust, and then the second mate who 'ad tipped 'im the wink followed us out unconcerned-like and 'anded Bill the mattress rolled up in a sack.

''Ere you are, Bill,' 'e says.

'Much obliged, sir,' says Bill, and 'is 'ands trembled so as 'e could 'ardly 'old it, and 'e made to go off afore Jimmy come on deck.

Then that fool of a mate kept us there while 'e made a little speech. Twice Bill made to go off, but 'e put 'is 'and on 'is arm and kept 'im there while 'e told 'im 'ow he'd always tried to be liked by the men, and 'ad generally succeeded, and in the middle of it up popped Master Jimmy.

He gave a start as he saw the bag, and 'is eyes opened wide, and then as we walked forward 'e put 'is arm through

Bill's and called 'im all the names 'e could think of.

'You'd steal the milk out of a cat's saucer,' 'e says; 'but mind, you don't leave this ship till I've got my share.'

'I meant it for a pleasant surprise for you, Jimmy,' says Bill, trying to smile.

'I don't like your surprises, Bill, so I don't deceive you,' says the boy. 'Where are you going to open it?'

'I was thinking of opening it in my bunk,' says Bill. 'The perlice might want to examine it if we took it through the dock. Come on, Jimmy, old man.'

'Yes; all right,' says the boy, nodding 'is 'ead at 'im. 'I'll stay up 'ere. You might forget yourself, Bill, if I trusted myself down there with you alone. You can throw my share up to me, and then you'll leave the ship afore I do. See?'

'Go to blazes,' says Bill; and then, seeing that the last chance 'ad gone, we went below, and 'e chucked the bundle in 'is bunk. There was only one chap down there, and arter spending best part o' ten minutes doing 'is hair 'e nodded to us and went off.

Half a minute later Bill cut open the mattress and began to search through the stuffing, while I struck matches and watched 'im. It wasn't a big mattress and there wasn't much stuffing, but we couldn't seem to see that money. Bill went all over it ag'in and ag'in, and then 'e stood up and looked at me and caught 'is breath painful.

'Do you think the mate found it?' 'e says, in a 'usky voice.

We went through it ag'in, and then Bill went half-way up the fo'c's'le ladder and called softly for Jimmy. He called three times, and then, with a sinking sensation in 'is stummick, 'e went up on deck and I follered 'im. The boy was nowhere to be seen. All we saw was the ship's cat 'aving a wash and brush-up afore going ashore, and the skipper standing aft talking to the owner.

We never saw that boy ag'in. He never turned up for 'is box, and 'e didn't show up to draw 'is pay. Everybody else was there, of course, and arter I'd got mine and come outside I see pore Bill with 'is back up ag'in a wall, staring 'ard at the second mate, who was looking at 'im with a kind smile, and asking 'im 'ow he'd slept. The last thing I saw of Bill, the pore chap 'ad got 'is 'ands in 'is trousers pockets, and was trying 'is hardest to smile back.

ABOUT TERRY O'BRIEN

Terry O'Brien is an academic with three decades of experience in teaching language and communication skills in India and abroad. He also headed a college under the auspices of the University of Delhi.

A prolific writer, with several books to his credit, Terry O'Brien is a reputed professional motivational speaker and a quizmaster.